I0566135

MY LIFE, BY RUSHIE

MY LIFE, BY RUSHIE

A Dog's Tale

With the Assistance of

FRED EVANS

Illustrated by Suzanna Dikker

THE BORGO PRESS

An Imprint of Wildside Press LLC

MMIX

Copyright © 2009 by Fred Evans
Interior illustrations Copyright © 2009 by Suzanna Dikker

All rights reserved.
No part of this book may be reproduced in any form
without the expressed written consent
of the author and publisher.

www.wildsidebooks.com

FIRST EDITION

CONTENTS

Author's Foreword

An autobiography by a dog? I know you're thinking that's preposterous. Who ever heard of a dog telling her own story? While unusual, I assure you-dog's honor-this is my story. My thoughts have been faithfully transcribed in this book.

To the skeptical reader, I'll be the first to admit that there are good reasons for the scarcity of canine literature. Paws are a major issue. It's hard to hold a pen, and almost impossible to type.

Although dogs can understand human (and some of us have a large vocabulary), it is our inability to speak human that is the major obstacle in the development of canine literature. Not only does it rule out dictation, because all literature is written in human, most dogs don't even consider recording their experiences. Dogs may think about careers as herders, guards, hunters, and companions but rarely as writers. In fact, writing this autobiography never crossed my mind until by chance I happened on to the diary kept by my human father, D.[1] In his diary, D described particular events of my life. As I read the diary, I was shocked at how profoundly M&D, who love me dearly and whom I love in return, misunderstood me.

Given my privileged upbringing and advanced education (I have graduated from two obedience schools, but was largely home schooled), I thought, "Rushie, you have an obligation to yourself and to future generations to set the record straight." My intention, first and foremost, is to tell my story, but in doing so I hope to make a small contribution to human understanding of dogs.

For readers of a literal bent, I did not actually write this book–not in the sense of putting pen to paper or typing on a laptop. (I don't ask the reader to believe that I miraculously grew fingers and opposable thumbs.) I used a rather simple literary device common among celebrities and important historical figures: I told my story to someone who could

---

[1] My human parents consist of Fred Evans, my father, and Natalie West my mother. Our family is close and I consider their relatives my relatives and their friends my friends. As I grew up, however, I ceased calling them "Mom" and "Dad" and referred to them instead as "M" and "D." I'm not totally sure why I did this, certainly not because I thought less of them as an adult than as a puppy. Perhaps it was because of the security, navigation, and other responsibilities I had implied a more equal relationship than is typical between a human and a dog. In life I began calling them M and D about the age of two. In the book I refer to them as M and D throughout.

write it for me. I chose D as my ghostwriter because over the years we've developed a very special ability to communicate.

He's transcribed my thoughts faithfully, if not always eloquently. I'd have preferred a better writer, but one does not choose one's parents, and I thank him for giving me the opportunity to express my views.

The reader will note that the book's format is unique for an autobiography in that it isn't written entirely by me. I first quote relevant portions of D's diary and then add my comments. I do this because it documents the frequent miscommunication between dogs and humans while allowing me to tell the reader about my interesting and unusual life.

Although the book begins with my first memories as a puppy, it was written over the past two years, beginning just six months after I discovered D's diary entries and ending with this Foreword.

To all of the dog owners who read this I hope you enjoy my autobiography and learn something about your dog in the process. To all of the dogs who will never read this but nevertheless will benefit, you may thank me at the Rainbow Bridge.

White Rush

February 6, 2006

A Note from the Author's Assistant

Helping Rushie write her autobiography has been an amazing experience. She is nothing if not an exacting taskmaster. On weekends we began the day at 6:30 A.M., sharp. I never needed to set my alarm. Rushie woke me with a gentle paw to the shoulder, which became less and less gentle until I actually got out of bed. She monitored my progress as I showered, dressed, ate breakfast and read the paper. She listened attentively while I commented on the day's news. After I finished my cereal, Rushie licked the remaining milk from the bowl and we went to work.

When we began the project we lived in Fresno, and we would move from the kitchen to the den where she would guard the house and dictate while I typed. On weekends we usually worked four hours straight. Rushie's powers of concentration and ability to multitask were impressive. It was a side of her I had not known previously.

During the week we would write in the evening before dinner. These weren't as intense as the weekend sessions, but were nonetheless productive. About a year into the book, we moved to Northridge, California. Rushie's health began to deteriorate rapidly. She slowed physically, but not mentally. Through sheer determination she forged ahead on the book, completing it just before she died.

Start to finish completing the first draft took two years. At the conclusion we both felt a great sense of accomplishment. And by working together so closely for so long, I felt that I had a far more profound and intimate understanding of Rushie than previously. Our bond was closer than ever and based on a new level of mutual respect.

I'll never forget when Rushie first became aware of my diary. One evening my wife, Natalie, and I were talking about how Rushie had refused to walk with her earlier that day. Natalie was exasperated. I laughed and said I thought I'd add the incident to my diary. I went to the study, retrieved the diary, returned to the living room and began to read some of the previous entries about Rushie out loud. Natalie and I were having a great time at Rushie's expense when I noticed Rushie sitting upright looking at me sternly. After reading a few entries I took the diary back to the study, made the entry about Rushie's refusal to walk with Natalie that day and returned to the living room.

Later when we sat for dinner Natalie noticed that Rushie hadn't joined us. This was very unusual. She called Rushie. Nothing. She started looking around the house (did she somehow get locked outside?) and finally found her in the den.

Natalie called, "Fred. Come here. You have to see this!" I walked in to see Rushie sitting on the chair staring at my diary, as it lay open on the desk. "Did you give Rushie permission to read your diary?" she asked. We laughed and walked back into the living room while Rushie stayed put. Twenty minutes later Rushie joined us, but seemed unusually subdued.

I couldn't stop thinking about Rushie's reaction to my diary. Then one evening Natalie and I were talking during dinner at our favorite Japanese restaurant. The conversation kept coming back to Rushie and the diary. We wondered what she would say in response to some of the entries. "Why don't you write a book that features Rushie's responses to your diary entries?" Natalie suggested. "Let her tell her side of the story." The idea for *My Life* was born.

As I proceeded to write the book, I began to wonder, and still do, whose idea it really was. At first, there was no question in my mind that it was Natalie's idea. Then I began to wonder where Natalie got the idea. Could it have been from Rushie?

When I first started to write *My Life*, I would look at Rushie sitting in front of the window guarding the house and watching me write. I tried to imagine what she might be thinking and what her reactions might have been to certain situations. The writing was slow and not very convincing. Gradually, her personality began to reveal itself to me. I could imagine exactly what Rushie was thinking and the words began to flow. Whenever I lacked for ideas I'd look at Rushie and ask out loud what she thought. She'd look me directly in the eyes and the ideas would come. I know this sounds fantastic, but it's true.

It is also true, as Rushie says in her foreword, that although I did the physical writing, this is Rushie's story—told by her. I hope you enjoy reading it as much as we did writing it.

Fred Evans

February 6, 2007

BOOK ONE

THE EARLY YEARS: GROWING UP (HUMAN)

Book One tells my story from my first memories
as a puppy to our move to Fresno, California
when I was three years old. I describe my
friendship with Big Red, the sports I invented
and play, some of my many adventures, including my first disastrous exposure to water, and
how I chose a career in household security.
These were my formative years—a time when I
began to separate myself from the canine world
to become a part of the human world.

Diary: *January 26, 1992*. We have a new addition to the family–a wire fox terrier puppy. Since her arrival, I've been so busy I haven't had a chance to keep up with my diary. Now is the time to catch up.

Seven tiny puppies were born early in the morning on December 10, 1991, in Cheney, Washington. We learned about one of those little miracles of nature five weeks later on January 14, 1992.

On Monday, January 13, I was sitting in my office suffering from the post-Christmas blues. My mind wandered and I began to think about dogs.

Natalie had been talking seriously about getting a dog ever since we moved to Spokane. For most of my life I've had a dog and thought someday I'd get another. But we both work long hours and I didn't think it would be right to get a dog just to leave it at home all day. Latchkey dogs end up like latchkey kids: stubborn, rebellious, and unhappy. Getting a dog wouldn't be fair to the dog. Natalie had a cat, Big Red, who was 25 pounds of muscle, sinew and red fur. That was enough, I thought.

We moved to Spokane in September 1988. We were excited about the move not only because of my new job–I had been appointed dean of the College of Business at Eastern Washington University–but also because we'd be closer to my son, Freddy, who lived in Seattle with his mother.

As it turned out, Freddy, now a teenager, thought Spokane was boring and preferred Seattle and his friends to Spokane and us. Natalie and I were now virtual empty nesters. Quickly, Natalie's desire for a dog strengthened and my resistance weakened. Since our Spokane house has plenty of room for a cat and a dog, why not both, she reasoned. As is typical in our relationship, when Natalie and I disagree about something important to her, she eventually prevails. This was no exception.

A few days later I was telling a friend at work that we were thinking about getting a fox terrier. He told me about Leslie, who also works at the university and breeds fox terriers as a hobby. When I called her that afternoon, she told me she had a litter of pups at home and said she would bring them to work if we were interested. I told her that we were and she brought them the next day. We met at a conference room near the woman's office. When we walked in, there was a cardboard box in the middle of the floor with four puppies–two boys and two girls–clamoring around inside. They were tiny balls of fur, barely five weeks old. Leslie told us that in the past week three puppies had been sold and these four were all that remained out of the litter. If we weren't already sure we would take one of the puppies home, the possibility that they would all be gone if we waited sealed our resolve.

She took the puppies out of the box and put them on the floor. They scrambled around, playing with each other and exploring the new world of the conference room. They were absolutely adorable. One, white with black spots and a tan patch on her head, was especially active. She climbed over the others and seemed to dominate the scene.

We fell in love with that little bundle of fur. I quickly wrote a check for $300 and we took her home.

Rushie: I was born on a cold winter day in Cheney, Washington on December 10, 1991. As far as I know my birth mother and father did not give me a name.

My first memories are of a big yard where my brothers and sisters (I had six of them, three brothers and three sisters) and I played. We didn't have much contact with humans and weren't allowed in the house. Even though it was winter, I don't remember ever being cold. We had a nice, heated corner of the garage where we slept. I can remember cuddling next to my brothers and sisters and drinking my mother's milk. I was warm and cozy during those cold winter nights.

My mother was so proud of us. She and my father would play with us, and we'd scramble around the garage floor and tumble out onto the lawn.

I guess growing up in Spokane, as I did, gave me a preference for cool weather. I was never able to get used to the heat in California. But more about that later.

After a month or so I noticed that my family was mysteriously shrinking. First one of my sisters was gone. Then, one of my brothers disappeared. By five weeks there were only four of us. It seemed very strange and it made me curious and a little nervous. Where did they go? Would I soon be alone? Would I disappear next?

We were playing in the garage as usual one morning when the lady (I later learned that her name was Leslie) came in and put my two brothers, my sister and me into a big box and closed the lid. It was dark and the box kept moving up and down and sideways. Every time we tried to stand the box would move and we'd fall down. Flopping around in the dark like that was fun, but also a bit scary. Then I felt the box plop down on something solid and the movement stopped. I heard one door shut, then another. Next, I heard the sound of what I now know was a car engine starting and felt a lurching motion as we began to move. I remember that I liked the feeling. Somehow, the hum of the tires and the gentle sway as the car moved down the road was relaxing. I fell asleep.

I awoke with a start when we stopped. I stood up and then fell down as the box lurched suddenly. A few minutes later the box hit the floor with a thud, and I fell again. Then, someone opened the lid and I could see that we were in a big room with lots of light. One by one, Leslie lifted us out of the box and placed us on the shiny tile floor. We didn't know where we were or who was there with us, and we didn't care. We just wanted to have fun, and this was an opportunity we couldn't pass up. We ran, growled, and tumbled over each other.

Then two people I had never seen before began to play with us. After a while they picked me up and petted me, leaving my brothers and sister playing on the floor. A few minutes later, Leslie put my sister and two brothers in the box and carried it out the door. I didn't know it at the time, but I would never see them again.

As I watched the box being carried through the door I that realized I was alone with two strangers. They seemed nice enough, but where was my mother? Where were my brothers and sisters? Who would I cuddle with? What would I eat? I was anxious and frightened.

Diary: *January 26, 1992 (continued)*. Natalie carried our as-yet-to-be-named dog in her arms to the car and held her close her as I drove. By the time we got home we both realized we were totally unprepared for this new addition to the family. I went to the store to buy food, dog dishes, a dog box for her to sleep in, and some toys for her to play with. I couldn't wait to get back home and see how our new puppy was doing.

Rushie: I remember going home with these two strangers to this big house. The nice woman picked me up and held me in her arms. She was warm and cuddly, and I felt safe as she carried me outside and into the cold. We walked up to a car, the man opened the door and the lady and I got inside. Then, the man opened the other door and sat behind the steering wheel, started the engine, and we began to move. I remembered that it was the same pleasant feeling that I had when I was in the box a couple of hours earlier. I liked the motion and the hum of the tires, and this time I could see trees and houses go by as we drove down the road. After a while my eyes started to get heavy and I fell asleep.

I awoke as the car slowed and turned into a driveway. I got nervous when we stopped. Everything was new and strange. The lady carried me into the house. I'd never been in a house before and was excited to see what was inside.

The house seemed very big. My most vivid memory was that it had lots of slippery wood floors that were hard to walk on. I was scared and excited. I remember wanting to see everything, and thought how much fun it would be to explore this new house. I guess I've always loved to explore new things, especially houses. M does, too, and we both enjoy going through model homes.

After a few minutes I had my first encounter with Big Red. I ran down the hall and slid to a stop when I saw a large creature with thick red fur. It looked something like a dog, but had a very different smell. He was big-almost as big as my mother. I thought he might want to play. As I ran up to him, he stood up. His ears were flat and his back was arched. He made a hissing sound that stopped me in my tracks. As young and inexperienced as I was, I quickly understood that he did not want to play. "Oh well," I thought, "I have lots more exploring to do anyway."

The best part of being in this new house was trying to figure out where everything was. There were so many rooms with so much stuff in them. And I remember thinking that I needed to see everything right away, because I'd probably be going home soon and wouldn't have much time to explore.

But I didn't go home. Gradually, over a period of weeks, I realized that this was my new home and these were my new parents.

Looking back on these events as an adult, I realize that for this new relationship to work, we all needed to make some adjustments. The first night illustrates how these adjustments would be made.

Diary: *January 28, 1992*. The first night with our new puppy was quite an experience. She is so cute and cuddly, but definitely has a mind of her own. Natalie wanted to hold her in her arms, like a baby. She submitted for a while, and then struggled to get loose to continue her explorations. Curiosity overwhelmed her; she wanted to see everything.

About 6:00 p.m. I fed her some warm milk and canned puppy food. She seemed hungry, and circled the food and sniffed it, but wouldn't eat. We couldn't figure out why. After much coaxing and cajoling, we finally left the room. To our surprise after we left she began to eat, but even then very slowly and cautiously.

Rushie: By evening I was getting hungry. They put out the food: warm milk in one bowl and some sort of ground up, mashed-together meat in another. Then they just stood there watching...and watching. I hardly knew these people! But I was hungry. I hadn't had anything to eat for hours.

Not wanting to be rude, I walked up to the

food, sniffed it and stepped back, hoping they would take the hint and leave. But they didn't. So I turned around and looked at them, then at the food. I walked away, trying to get them to follow, but they just stood there. For a while it was a standoff. Finally, I think they got bored watching and walked into the other room.

I sniffed the milk. It had a strange but not unpleasant odor. I took a taste. It wasn't nearly as good as I was used to, but I drank it anyway. Because it was there, I sniffed the disgusting stuff in the other bowl. Still not sure, I took a small bite, carried it out to the living room, placed it on the rug and sniffed it again. It seemed okay, and I ate a small piece. It tasted better than it looked. I returned to the bowl and took a few more bites, then walked back to the living room to let them know that I was done.

M&D think my eating habits are unusual. And I guess they are, at least for a dog. But I've never liked to eat when there is a lot of commotion or noise or when people are watching me. I just don't understand why some dogs gulp their food, as if they hadn't eaten for days. Frankly, I think it is pretty crude. Labs are the worst. They devour their food without even tasting it and pay for it by getting fat. I'm concerned about my figure and have always tried to stay trim by watching what I eat.

Diary: *January 28, 1992 (continued)*. After dinner and all the excitement of the day, our exhausted little puppy fell asleep in Natalie's lap. She'd wake occasionally, look around with half closed eyes, and then fall back to sleep. Natalie was in heaven. You'd have thought she was holding her own baby. In a way she was.

I carried the dog box I'd bought that day in from the garage and put it on the floor next to our bed. I put in fluffy blankets and a pillow to make her comfortable and even a clock that ticked to lull her to sleep.

Our resolution from the time we started thinking about getting a dog was that a dog's place was beside the bed not in it. We both got ready for bed, brought the puppy in from the living room, put her in the box, and shut the wire door. She seemed so tired that we both thought she'd sleep through the night. Not 30 seconds after we turned out the lights, she started to whimper. Natalie got up a couple of times to comfort her, but as soon as she got back in bed, the puppy would start to cry again.

After no more than fifteen minutes, we gave up and brought her up on the bed. She immediately curled up in Natalie's arms and went to sleep. When I woke up in the morning, she was under the covers nestled up against Natalie's stomach. Natalie had her new baby and the puppy had her new mother.

Rushie: I know now that they love me, but I wasn't sure at the time. Think of my situation. I was away from home for the first time in my life, my brothers and sisters were nowhere around, and I hadn't seen my mom for the longest time.

I'll have to admit, when I got tired, being held by M was comforting. There always has been something about her lap that fits me. I've tried to sleep on D's lap occasionally, but his legs are too far apart and hard and boney; M's lap is soft and comfortable.

Anyway, that night I was excited, but also lonely and confused. You know how small children are when they get too tired? They get cranky and cry. Well, that's how I was. For the first time in my life I felt alone.

It was getting late and I was tired. I remember being on M's warm lap, dreaming that I was back home with my brothers and sisters. I don't even remember D carrying me down the hall to the bedroom. But I was instantly awake when he laid me down on the floor of this cage with locks on the door! Can you believe that two people who thought they wanted a puppy would actually be so heartless as to make her sleep by herself on the cold floor, while they slept together in a warm and comfortable bed? Besides, who could possibly sleep with a clock ticking all night?

I started to cry.

Finally, after several long hours (Fifteen minutes? Hardly!) M picked me up and took me to bed. That's when I first began to feel that I belonged. M was warm and soft and I could feel her love. As a puppy I liked nothing more than to go to bed and snuggle up next to her.

The next night when I came to bed I noticed that the stupid cage was gone. We were starting to adjust.

Diary: *January 30, 1992.* We named our new dog White Rush or Rushie for short. Most of the time all we see is a white blur as she rushes from place to place. After a few days, we thought that perhaps we should have named her Rushie the Ripper–when she's not rushing she seems intent on chewing anything and everything she can get her teeth on, including human flesh. Is there anything sharper than a puppy's teeth? Natalie and I have puncture wounds all over our hands and arms.

The other day I commented to the owner of Wyre Crest Kennels, where they breed fox terriers for show, about how berserk Rushie seemed to be. He just shrugged and told me that was one of the charms of the breed. "There's a reason why they're nicknamed fox *terrors*," he said.

Rushie: I like the name White Rush. It's elegant and distinctive. D always calls me Rushie, which is a good nickname. M calls me a variety of things, including Rushie, Winklie, Winklie Bobo, Pewee Puppin, and lots of other names. At first I was confused. She'd call me by a name I hadn't heard before and expect me to respond. Well, if I hadn't heard the name before, how could I know she was talking to me? After a while I got used to her name-calling and responded to each of her nicknames. One time I counted, and she had 25 different names for me. I don't mind the nicknames when it's just between the two of us, but calling me Winklie Bobo or Pewee Puppin in front of strangers is embarrassing. Who would take a dog named Winklie Bobo seriously?

As for the teeth, what can I say? I was a puppy! Maybe D had forgotten that puppies have loads of energy and not much judgment. I play with M&D every day, and have as long as I can remember. When I play I bite, because that is what dogs do. As I got older I learned to bite more gently, after all I'm not trying to hurt anyone. But as a puppy you don't know how hard to bite or how sharp your teeth are. It's a learning process. Good parents learn to be patient, D.

Luckily, my adult teeth aren't as sharp as my baby teeth were. This makes it easier to bite and play without hurting. Cats, on the other hand, have sharp teeth even when they are adults. Plus they have really sharp claws. One time Big Red bit me on the nose and made it bleed. It really hurt! After that when I wanted to play with Red I'd jump on him when he wasn't looking and quickly move out of reach. Cats can be pretty moody, and you have to be careful. Despite this, Big Red and I soon became good friends.

After three weeks I began to feel like this was my home.

Diary: *February 16, 1992.* Over the past several weeks Rushie has become part of the family. She's growing every day and really developing her own unique (if slightly eccentric) personality.

Rushie: Those first few weeks were a blur. I got to know and love M and D. I explored every corner of the house and most of the yard. I enjoyed being a puppy. I was brash and not afraid of anything. The world was filled with new sights and smells wherever I went.

I especially loved riding in the car, and M took me with her everywhere. She'd go to the store or cleaners and leave me in the front seat. I'd usually go to sleep and wake up excited when she returned. Sometimes she'd even bring me a treat. When we drove, I'd sit on her lap and look out the window. I pride myself on my sense of direction, and even when I was only three months old I knew exactly where I was at all times.

Another remarkable thing about me is how quickly I learned English. I learned my name in one day. Shortly after that I learned "come" and "no" (though I've never paid much attention to these commands). Every day I learned more words. By the time I was two years old I understood most of what M&D said. I think M&D realized that I understood everything, and they often told me what they were thinking. When D came home after work, he'd tell M and me about his day, and I knew if he had a good day or a bad day and why. (If he had a really bad day, I'd sit next to him on the sofa and try to make him feel better.) My frustration wasn't my ability to understand English but my inability to speak it. I learned to communicate through gestures and sign language, but, try as I might, I simply couldn't get my mouth to form words. Gradually, I gave up trying to speak and concentrated on communicating through sign language and facial expressions.

Diary: *February 23, 1992*. Rushie is so adorable. Natalie sits in front of her computer at home for much of the day writing while I am at the office. Rushie either sleeps on her lap or gets up on her shoulders, with her front legs draped around one side of her neck and her back legs around the other. From her shoulder perch, Rushie can watch Natalie type on the computer. I came home for lunch the other day and took a picture of the two of them in the den "working."

Rushie: I really like being around M, and when I was little I didn't let her out of my sight. Most mornings, D would go to work and M and I would stay home. I'd follow her everywhere, even into the bathroom. I'd wait on the bathroom floor while she showered and help her dry off by licking the water off her legs when she got out. That was the fun part. Waiting for her to put on her make-up took a long time and wasn't much fun.

I've always thought M is pretty. She has blond hair (like the hair on my head), she is tall and thin with big, brown eyes (also like me). She has a good complexion and nice, smooth skin, so I could never figure out why she spends so much time putting on make-up in the morning. She tells me that she takes pride in her appearance-I do as well-but I look good with a bath and comb every couple of weeks and a trim every couple of months. If someone is naturally pretty, like M and me, why spend all that time primping?

After M finishes her shower and puts on her make-up she usually has something to eat. I've always tried to eat like M. She eats slowly and savors each bite. She never eats too much. D, on the other hand, eats a lot of food fast.

The only thing that keeps him thin is that he exercises so much. M's eating habits are much more dignified, in my opinion.

I've loved cheese for as long as I can remember, but before I take a bite of anything—even cheese—I want to make sure it's fit to eat. So I give it several good sniffs to make sure it's not spoiled. I then take it very gently between my teeth and taste it carefully before chewing and swallowing. And, as I already mentioned, I really hate eating in front of people. So I usually go to another room to eat. I think the way I eat is far superior to the way D and most dogs eat. What if someone gave you bad food and you just gulped it down? Or what if—God forbid—someone tried to poison you? Then you'd get sick and be sorry you hadn't taken the time to test the food before you ate it.

I've always believed in learning from experience. Why repeat mistakes if you don't have to? Over the years I've discovered ten "Rushie Rules" that I live by. They work for me and they will work for you.

Thinking about how to eat properly was how I discovered **Rushie Rule 1:** *Never gulp your food.* Taste first; make sure the food is fit to eat. Always eat slowly, leaving some food in the dish in case you get hungry later. Never overeat! Overeating can cause a stomachache and make you fat. As D says, obesity is a big problem in this country. Don't be a part of the problem!

After breakfast, M would go into the study and sit at her desk. By this time, it was mid-morning and I would be getting sleepy. M fixed a bed in the room so I could sleep while she worked, but I didn't use it that much at first because I would rather be in her lap. One day I decided to climb up on her shoulders. I discovered that lying with my legs draped around her neck and my back on the top of the chair was pretty comfortable. I could look down and watch her type her stories or close my eyes and take a nap. I did this for a long time until I started to notice that M's shoulders were getting smaller and smaller. Gradually I quit lying on them. One day, remembering how comfortable it used to be, I got up there again. It was hard to balance, but I was determined to stay. I must have dozed off. Just as I did M moved and I fell off her shoulders and onto the floor-thud! It was a real shock. I tried to get onto her shoulders a time or two after that, but I always felt like I was going to fall. Finally, I gave up and slept on my bed on the floor or on M's lap.

One day, M moved the sofa from one side of the room to the other. The sofa was now where my bed had been, with its back to a window that looked out on the front yard and street beyond. At first I was irritated that she had moved my bed, but then I realized that I could climb up on the back of the sofa and look out the window. This helped pass the time while M worked.

Gradually I realized that from this vantage point I could see any would-be intruders. So I

began watching for them and barking when someone came too close. I soon realized I was good
at this and it interested me. It was my first
exposure to what would become a long career in
the security business.

When I was a puppy, M and I were inseparable.
When she wrote, I was in the room with her.
When she gardened I went outside and helped.
When she drove the car, I sat on her lap and
navigated.

Diary: *March 2, 1992.* Natalie takes that puppy wherever she goes.
One of my colleagues at work calls her the "dog lady" because you
just don't see Natalie without Rushie. Yesterday, Rushie slipped
away from Natalie in the busy supermarket parking lot. She didn't
think she'd ever get her back in the car. She ran away every time
Natalie tried to pick her up. She was sure that Rushie was going to
get hit by a car.

Rushie. Yeah, I remember that. I was feeling
pretty good that day, even more full of energy
than usual. When M opened the car door I realized that I was big enough to jump to the
ground. So I did. That was kind of neat, new
sights and smells. M was acting pretty
strange, though. She was yelling and running
toward me. At first I was a little scared-I
didn't want to get a spanking-so I ran. Then,
it seemed like a game. She'd bob and I'd
weave. She'd chase and I'd run. I was really
having fun! M would try to trap me and I'd get
out of it. Then a woman I never saw before
snuck up from behind, grabbed me, and handed
me to M. Fun over. Boy, was M mad! She scolded
me all the way home.

I realize now that I scared M and that it was dangerous to run around a parking lot like that, especially when I didn't know how much it can hurt to get hit by a car. But, give me a break; I'm not the only one who makes mistakes.

One time, M took me to the market and left me in the car on a very cold winter day. At first I was okay; I usually don't mind the cold. I don't know why she was taking so long in the store, but the car got colder and colder. Here I am on the seat with no blanket and no heater. All I could do was curl up in a ball and shiver. When M finally came back to the car and saw me shivering, she grabbed me and held me close until I was warm.

My point? Anyone can make mistakes. But when I read D's diary, there's no mention of my half freezing in the parking lot that winter because M forgot about me. He only mentions how I jumped out of the car and wouldn't come when I was called.

I'm not making excuses. I'm just pointing out the double standard. Looking back, it's one of the things that bug me most. M's got a big family with lots of little nieces and nephews. Those kids can jump on me and pull my ears and scream and yell and everything is hunky dory. But if I react with even the smallest growl, I'm a Bad Girl. Or how about eating at the table? I get food all mashed up in a bowl, usually straight out of a can, while they sit at the table eating one gourmet meal after another. If I ask for some of their food, I'm told to stop "begging."

Is it unfair? Yes. Is it something that I alone face? No. This is how humans treat dogs. If this autobiography accomplishes anything, I hope that it will bring some attention to the double standard that humans apply to dogs.

After a few months I started becoming more confident and less dependent on M&D. This is a normal part of growing up, but apparently it was a big surprise to them.

Diary: *April 10, 1992.* Rushie is turning out to be a great little dog, but boy does she have a mind of her own! She walks around the house like the resident princess and comes when called only when it suits her. Most of the time her independence is endearing, but sometimes it is really frustrating–like when she got out of the car in the parking lot again, or when she hides under the bed and won't come out. Try to grab her and she growls.

Rushie: Princess? Please. Look, I hang around M&D all day every day. Whenever they want to do something I'm supposed to be right there, tail wagging, perky, and anxious to do whatever. I'm pretty considerate most of the time. I've never turned M down for a ride in the car–not once! And when D comes home from work I jump up and go to the door to greet him the second I hear the garage door open.

I think I'm pretty cooperative, but I'm a fox terrier, not a French poodle, and I have my own interests. For instance, why shouldn't I be able to get out of the car and explore the parking lot while M shops? I wouldn't have gotten lost. Yet every time I got out of the car in the parking lot she went through the same routine: yelling, cajoling, chasing, and scolding. I finally decided it's just not worth it. After the second time, I never jumped out of the car again. I call that flexibility.

Let me explain the "hiding-under-the-bed" issue. By the time I learned that technique I was about five months old, early adolescence in dog years. Well, you know how teenagers need their space. M, bless her heart, can be so clingy, and sometimes I just needed to get away. I tried everything. I hid upstairs on the couch in the entertainment room, on the bed in Freddy's room (Freddy is D's son and my stepbrother), on the sofa in the living room, and even in that old dog box that D put in the laundry room. She'd always find me, wake me, grab me and put her hands all over me. Don't get me wrong; I like being petted as much as the next dog, but sometimes enough is enough. So I finally tried hiding under the bed in the guest room. It was dark and cozy and comfortable and reminded me of a foxhole. I knew that M was too big to get under there with me. Good idea, I thought.

Well, the way M carried on, you'd think I'd run away from home. After she finally found me (it took her quite a while, I'm pleased to say) she reached under the bed and pulled my tail to get me to come out. If a growl is ever called for, it's when someone pulls your tail. That slowed her down for about a minute. Then she started to pester me again. Finally, I gave up and came out.

I went back under the bed a few more times, but it was always such a battle that I finally gave up. After that when I needed to be alone I retreated to the dog box they kept in the laundry room, which didn't seem to bother her as much. I found that just lying down, pretending that I was asleep, and making a slight "guurrr" if anyone tried to pet me was more effective than hiding. Once I developed what I call the "Guurrr Technique" they began to give me more space. I use it all the time now.

That's when I discovered **Rushie Rule 2:** *Communicate, communicate, communicate!* If something bothers you, say so. A good relationship requires open communication. Dogs are notorious for being doormats. Good dog/human relations require two-way communication-dogs should express themselves and humans should listen.

Not long after being adopted, I heard about Tristie, a wire fox terrier D had when he was younger. D was always comparing her to me. Here's an example-one of the few in which I get the best of the comparison.

Diary: *April 20, 1992.* Rushie is living up to the reputation of wildness that fox terriers have and deserve.

Tristie, the fox terrier my first wife and I had, also was a menace when she was young. We both worked and Tristie was home alone all day. She chewed everything, including-and especially-the furniture. She chewed the arm off our stuffed leather chair. Twice. She chewed both arms off the sofa. And she chewed the backs off all of my books. When we left her at my parents' house one day, she chewed a hole in the wall behind her bed. She was a maniac until she was two years old.

Rushie has an equal amount of energy. If we don't take her for a walk every day, and if I don't throw her toy for a half hour, she has so much energy that she can't sleep at night.

Two things keep her from being as destructive as Tristie. First, we buy her rawhide chews. She loves them and devours at least one big one every night. Anytime she gets too much nervous energy we give her a chew, which she attacks with relentless enthusiasm. Thank God we can buy huge packages cheaply at Costco. The other thing is that she won't eat food or even chew her rawhide when she is home alone. I think she misses us and goes on hold until we return. Anyway, she's never chewed any of our furniture. We feel lucky and are keeping our fingers crossed.

Rushie: When I was young I had so much energy I sometimes felt like I was tingling all over and I needed to do something, anything, to make it stop. Sometimes I would run around in circles until I couldn't run anymore. Other times I would chase Big Red. (The problem with chasing Red was that he could get irritable and had pretty sharp claws, so I had to be careful.)

Finally, I invented a game that D and I played almost every night. One day, D took me to a pet store and let me pick out a toy. I picked a red rubber ring that had a bump on it with a rattle inside. I'm not much for toys, but the ring toy intrigued me. When we got home I played with it in my mouth, tossed it into the air, and watched it bounce on the floor. Then D grabbed it and threw it down the hall. I raced after it, catching it before it stopped rolling. When I brought it back he tried to grab it from me. I held on and we played tug of war. Finally I let go and he threw it down the hall again. The ring toy game was born!

D and I played for at least half an hour every night before dinner. It was fun and it made me tired enough that I could sleep at night. I feel sorry for Tristie being left alone all day, and I can understand why she ate all of D's books. I hate to think of what my life would be like without my game, although I doubt I'd resort to eating books.

After first ignoring me, Big Red became more and more friendly. We'd fight occasionally, but most of the time we played and even took naps together. I came to love Big Red like a brother.

Diary: *April 29, 1992.* After a rocky start, Rushie and Big Red get along pretty well. Red likes to be on top of a high table in the living room with his feet over the edge. When Rushie tries to get him, he swats at her to keep her at bay. Rushie plays the game for a while, but soon gets frustrated and starts to bark, as if to say, "C'mon, Big Red, fight like a man." After a while Red will get down from the table and race down the hall, sounding every bit like a small horse, with Rushie in hot pursuit.

Rushie: I played with Big Red every day. In his prime he was pretty fast and strong. Plus he's a really good boxer. When he got on the table, and I tried to bite him (playfully, of course), he'd swipe at me with his paws. I never could get him. He was just too fast. I'd get frustrated and bark at him because he never let me win. If anything, barking made matters worse. He'd just look at me calmly and wait. And swipe.

Finally, I'd go to the far corner of the room and lie down as if I was going to sleep, but I wouldn't. I'd watch him out of the corner of my eye. He'd get down and start to walk across the room. That's when I'd run and pounce. Sometimes, I'd catch him and we'd roll around on the floor play fighting. Other times, he'd see me and run. I'd chase him down the hall, through the dining room, back through the living room, up the stairs and into the den where he'd hop up on the bar. When he thought I wasn't looking, he'd hop down and run back down the stairs and repeat the circuit. It was great fun. Eventually, we'd both get tired and take a nap together.

Although Red adjusted to me being a member of the household pretty quickly, M&D weren't quite as flexible, as this next entry illustrates.

Diary: *May 2, 1992*. Rushie's turning out to be really tough to house train. She'll go without an accident for a few days and then make two or three mistakes in a row. Sometimes we take her outside and: nothing. Then, not ten minutes later, she'll make a mistake in the house. I'm not sure why this is such a difficult concept for her to grasp.

Rushie: This is another sore subject. Big Red doesn't have to go outside to go to the bathroom, and neither do M&D. (Well, D goes outside occasionally, but that's usually on the weekends when he's working in the yard.) Yet, they expect me to go outside every time and in all kinds of weather. One time, the snow was so deep that when D opened the sliding glass door in the bedroom there was nowhere to go-the snow had drifted right up to the window. The wind was blowing, and the snow was flying. Every time I tried to climb up the drift I sunk in. Let me tell you-when you sink in the snow up to your stomach it makes it pretty hard to go to the bathroom. It was annoying and undignified. But my feelings didn't matter.

Another thing. I hate to admit this, but M&D are a bit weird about the whole toilet-training issue. Every time they let me out of the house to go, they stand around and watch. (How gross is that!?) Now going to the bathroom, especially number two, is disgusting even if no one is watching. (What I usually do when I have to go number two is to wait until the very last minute, stop whatever I'm doing, do it, and then leave immediately and hope nobody notices. It usually works.) It is really disgusting when one or two people are watching you go, and under those conditions sometimes I just can't. (M&D ought to try to go to the bathroom when someone is watching I'll bet they'd have trouble, too. There's a reason bathrooms have doors.)

After one of those unsuccessful visits outside with M&D watching and commenting on my every move, I came back into the house and tried to forget about the entire disgusting matter. Once (well, several times) I put it off too long and had to go immediately-no time to go outside. A mistake, I know, but what am I supposed to do? A few times I've thought that maybe going in the house like they do was okay. I learned over the years, however, that on this matter (as on many others) they have a double standard-it's okay for them to go in the house, but not for me. I've learned to live with it. I'm nothing if not adaptable.

One thing I like about Big Red is that he is dignified. They didn't expect Big Red to go out that snowy night. And I'm pretty sure he wouldn't have even if they told him to.

Another thing that is undignified is how M&D expect me to "obey."

Diary: *May 16, 1992*. Rushie is old enough now to mind, but doesn't. She comes when she is called only when she wants to but never because we want her to. Maybe five months is too young, but we haven't been able to teach her any tricks. It's hard to tell whether she doesn't get it or is just stubborn.

Rushie: Here we go again with the name-calling. Am I stubborn or stupid? What a thing to say! When you chose a fox terrier you should know that you were choosing a dog that can think for herself. Remember, D, you had a fox terrier before me. I don't see how you could forget. You told me enough times about how adorable and smart Tristie was. Think back. How different was Tristie from me? And you say I have a hard time learning things!

What you call stubbornness is really self-confidence. I know who I am and I know what I want to do. You could see this even when I was a puppy. Lots of other dogs just sit around thinking about how to make people feed, pet, or play with them. Not fox terriers, not me. Fox terriers were bred to go underground after a fox. It's a dangerous job. When you are down in that hole, it's just you and the fox. There's no place to run, and no place to hide. No one is down there with you telling you what to do. Hunters tell hunting dogs where to hunt; shepherds tell sheep dogs which sheep to herd; owners tell guard dogs when to attack. Fox terriers survive not by listening to others but by making their own decisions. Self-confidence and intelligence allow fox terriers to make the split-second decisions necessary for survival. Just because I don't actually hunt foxes doesn't mean that I have the personality of a poodle.

Want me to do tricks? Catch me in the right

mood, make it interesting, and I can learn just about anything. But try to push me around or make me do something just because you want me to and I'll fight back. Most dogs should be trained. Terriers should be educated.

Sorry about the lecture, D. Actually after two or three years you seemed to get the message. I'm not sure why it took so long. I could never tell if you were being stubborn or just didn't get it.

Which reminds me: The first obedience class M took me to was a complete disaster. After it was over, I tried to forget it ever happened.

Diary: *May 20, 1992.* Natalie signed Rushie up for obedience school, hoping to teach her rudimentary dog behavior like sit, stay, and come. Because Rushie is only five months old, Natalie tried to find a puppy training session, but none was available, so she enrolled her into a program for adolescent dogs. No luck. Rushie didn't like school, and after the second session, when Rushie hid under a chair and threw up, Natalie decided that enough was enough.

We didn't think about it at the time, but it was like enrolling a child in middle school instead of first grade. It was a waste of our time and traumatic for Rushie.

Rushie: Well, this was a little embarrassing. I went with M in the car one night and we ended up in this tiny room with a whole bunch of other people and dogs. This was the first time I had ever been around so many dogs at once. And I'll have to admit that other dogs make me nervous. You never know what they are going to do. I've never liked surprises. Dogs that move too fast or little kids that jump around worry me. I don't want to get bit or hurt, so I think the best policy is to be very careful in these situations.

Anyway, I was only five months old, and here they were sending me to a school for grown up dogs. Hello! Every one of those dogs was older and bigger than me, and they all looked really mean.

M wanted me to sit on her lap. But that didn't make any sense because the mean dogs that were growling could see me there. So, I thought the best thing to do was to get under the chair and hide behind M's legs. When I did and looked around I realized that the other dogs could still see me. A couple of them were straining at their leashes trying to attack. What if their leash broke or slipped out of their owner's hand? They could easily reach their head around the legs of the chair and bite me. These dogs looked mean. I was sure I'd have to fight for my life at any minute.

D wasn't even there. I always feel safest around him because he is used to handling difficult situations. (When I'm afraid D makes me feel safe. When I'm sick or sad or need help with something, I turn to M and she's always there for me.)

During this entire crisis, M kept saying, "It's okay, Rushie, don't worry, it'll be fine," etc., while I was trying to keep track of the dogs. I'm sorry, but when I'm a dangerous situation I don't have time to chat.

Finally, she picked me up and we left. I was relieved, but didn't completely relax until I got back home.

And do you know what? The next week M put me in the car and took me back to that place. When I got into the room and saw all those dangerous animals, I immediately hid under the chair. Looking around the room, I got so worried my stomach tightened into a knot and I threw up.

I was glad that I didn't have to go back to school again for a long time.

Just because I wasn't going to school doesn't mean I wasn't learning. I was bitten by the home security bug and began teaching myself how to guard the house, as this next diary entry explains.

Diary: *June 23, 1992.* I think Rushie has found her calling. After breakfast she joins Natalie in the study. But instead of sitting on her lap she sits on the back of the sofa that faces the window and guards the house. She is alert to all possible intruders. Cars that drive by too slowly or birds that land too close to the house warrant a low growl. The mail carrier deserves a fearsome bark-and-growl combination. And God forbid if a dog should wander into her yard! Hysterical barking and growling combinations ensue.

Rushie: I got into the security business by chance when M moved the sofa in the study next to the window. Before that the only time I ever was concerned about intruders was when someone knocked on the door. But once I was able to see what was in front of the house I immediately recognized the possibility of danger and the need to be prepared. Cars and dogs and people passed our house every day. The mail carrier came every morning and the refuse collector weekly. These were all potential threats to which M&D seemed oblivious.

Someone had to do something. I decided that it would be me. I taught myself to distinguish threats from diversions, and I developed a warning system. A soft growl is a Level One Alert, which indicates the need to pay attention; a growl with a single bark is a Level Two Alert, which warns that danger is a real possibility; a loud growl interspersed with rapid barking is a Level Three Alert, which means that an intruder is approaching; rapid, non-stop barking interspersed with deep growls is a Level Four Alert, unequivocally signaling that security has been breached and danger is imminent.

Of course, at six months of age even at my most vicious, I wasn't very intimidating. But I was learning and improving every day. Looking back, the best thing about taking responsibility for household security was that it gave me a purpose in life and made me feel that I was a contributing member of the family. It was a good decision, and I am proud of my accomplishments.

Important as my security contributions were, they did not protect me from being compared to Tristie.

Diary: *June 28, 1992*. Fox terriers are bred to be fearless. The role of the terrier was to finish off the foxes after the hounds had chased them into their holes. Not a job for the faint of heart.

Tristie wasn't afraid of anything. The only dog I ever saw her defer to was a pit bull. Rushie, however, is the world's biggest chicken, at least when it comes to other dogs (I don't know about foxes). Every time we take her for a walk and she sees another dog she gets nervous. She hides behind Natalie or me when a dog comes up to her. Big dogs, little dogs. It doesn't matter, she's afraid of them all. If a dog barks or growls and gets really aggressive, she yips and cries as if she thinks she's going to be eaten alive.

Recently we took Rushie on a walk past a neighbor's yard where a child was playing with a wind-up dog. The toy walked and made barking sounds. It scared Rushie to death! She jumped back and started pulling on her leash to go home. Finally, Natalie picked Rushie up to calm her. Then I picked the toy dog up and held it for her to sniff. Slowly she realized it wasn't a real dog, but still didn't want to get too close. The neighbors laughed and laughed. Frankly, I was embarrassed for her.

Rushie: Thanks, D, for another insight into your beloved Tristie. She must have been a wonderful dog. Too bad she's dead.

You don't understand. There are lots of evil dogs out there. The world can be a very dangerous place. I like to go for walks. I like to see the sights and smell the smells. I really like to smell where other dogs have been. Understand, I can tell a lot about other dogs this way. I don't actually need to meet them face-to-face.

When we see another dog on a walk, why can't you just keep walking? I can see; I can smell. Why do you have to take me so close to the dog that it could bite me? I play along and try to be a good sport. I sniff, but when they move too fast I think it is only prudent to get out of the way. You never can be too careful. Plus, I've heard that a lot of dogs have rabies. Why take a chance?

About that toy dog, put yourself in my place. I'm maybe five months old and 12 pounds soaking wet. Not exactly a fighting machine. I look to my left and see this dog walking toward me on legs that don't even bend. He's looking right at me with unblinking, beady black eyes, while barking ferociously. If Frankenstein had a dog this is how he would look. I don't see his owner anywhere. He's not on a leash. Next I see is this little kid running after the dog. Maybe the dog has eaten the kid's parents; maybe the dog will try to eat me, too.

I had to make a quick decision. My decision was to retreat. What's so wrong with that? I can walk anytime. Remember, prudence is a virtue.

Diary: *July 17, 1992*. Natalie told me that a statue scared our brave dog! She took Rushie to the nursery to buy some plants. They were walking down an aisle with rows of plants on each side. Tucked to one side was a statue of a sitting dog. When Rushie saw the statue she stopped, turned, and ran. Horrors. She was so upset that Natalie had to put her in the car before she could finish her shopping.

Rushie: That statue was very realistic. It was of a giant dog-I think it was supposed to be a pit bull-that looked like it was hiding behind some bushes waiting to ambush anyone who walked by. I was afraid it might attack M. I wanted to make sure she didn't get maimed.

I quickly realized it wasn't real. And I was never afraid for myself. I was concerned for M.

I am not a chicken, but I will admit that when I was young I did have a problem with other dogs, and I always wondered why. Over the years I've come to the conclusion that it may have something to do with my being taken from my canine parents at only five weeks of age. I've spent most of my life around humans and have never felt entirely comfortable around dogs. Sometimes I watch other dogs playing in the park, and I wish I could be like them-running and having fun without a care in the world. Try as I might, I never can. For one thing, I'm always thinking ahead and planning for what's coming next-I'm a control freak, I'll admit-so it's hard to just let loose and stay in the moment like most dogs. I also understand how humans behave and I'm comfortable around them. Dogs, on the other hand, can be fun loving one minute and vicious the next. They are hard to predict and it makes me nervous. Finally (excuse me if this sounds a little snotty), I am much smarter than most dogs, and I expect them to recognize this. Many don't. I don't blame them because, after all, they are just dogs, but that makes me want to be around them even less.

If I had to make a choice, I'd rather be the way I am-pretty, smart, and doing things most dogs wouldn't dream of, like writing my autobiography–than be a pal to every stray dog in the park.

My individuality is a continuing concern for M&D, and their double standard is a continuing concern for me, as this next entry illustrates.

Diary: *July 13, 1992.* More on the continuing saga of Rushie's toilet training issues. She's old enough now to not make mistakes, but still does. A lot of them. She'll go for a couple of weeks without an accident. Pretty soon either Natalie or I will remark about how good she's been, thinking she has finally gotten the message. Invariably, as soon as we comment she makes another mistake. The mistakes usually come in bunches. It's as if she's been good as long as she can and needs to get it out of her system. (Sorry for the dreadful pun.)

In fairness, when she needs to go outside she normally asks. But when she does she's so subtle that sometimes we don't even know she's asking. The other morning I was in the bathroom shaving. I'd let Rushie out as soon as we got up, but she apparently needed to go out again. She tiptoed into the bathroom, stood behind me, and touched my leg with her nose–so gently I barely noticed. Having fulfilled her responsibility she turned around and left the room–for the door, I guess.

Well, I didn't immediately pick up on her request. Rushie only asks once, usually at the very last minute. Not more than five minutes after she had nudged me, I finished shaving and walked to the kitchen to get coffee before dressing. As I walked to the kitchen I saw that she had pooped on the floor in front of the back door. Exasperated, I looked for and found her at work guarding the house and told her what a bad dog she was. She looked at me, guiltless and a bit irritated, as if to say, "Don't bother me now; I'm working."

Natalie blamed me for not paying attention. I blame Rushie for not being more assertive.

Rushie: This subject again!? I hate even to respond, but believe I must.

It's my fault? I'm to blame? Please! I walked into the bathroom and told you that I needed to go outside. You ignored me. I had no other choice. What am I supposed to do? I can't plan these trips; I just respond to nature's calls.

You, of all people, should understand the meaning of urgency. How many times have you gotten up in the morning, showered, dressed, eaten and started to back the car out of the garage only to suddenly stop the car, get out, and rush back into the house because you had to go to the bathroom? What if the door were locked, and you didn't have a key? What would you do?

The difference between us is that you can go in and out of the house whenever you want. Someone has to let me in and out. Ever think of installing a pet door?

As for being too subtle in telling you about my needs, may I remind you that I am a lady, and this is not something I want to herald so everyone knows that I HAVE TO GO TO THE BATH-ROOM! Think what you will, but on this subject I refuse to yield.

I've always liked my walks with M. But when D decided that I should go jogging with him I wasn't sure that I would like it. After a few times I was pretty sure it was a bad idea. Unfortunately, D can be very persistent.

Diary: *August 1, 1992.* Rushie just won't jog with me. At first, I thought that she might be too young; now she is older and strong enough to run with me, but she refuses. She doesn't enjoy it and is always trying to turn back or slow down. It's really disappointing. Running with my dog through the park would be so much fun and such good exercise for both of us.

Rushie: Well, I'm sorry I'm not perfect. Face it, D, jogging is boring. I like to go outside. I like the park. I like the smells. I like to see people and dogs (the latter from a safe distance). And I love to chase squirrels and birds. When I "jog" with you (I really should say when I "fast walk" with you) you don't let me do the fun things. I never get to slow down to smell the trees and shrubs. You run right by the squirrels and birds. It seems like all you care about is going to the park running around and coming back as fast as you can (which isn't very fast, I must say).

I try to be a good sport. Don't you think I know what is going to happen when you put on your running shoes and get the leash? I try to play along for the first ten minutes or so. When I slow down you should know that it is time to start doing things my way. You never take the hint. You just keep pulling harder on the leash and start yelling, "Rushie, come on! Rushie, hurry up!" Frankly, I get embarrassed when you yell like that.

Remember the time you were running headlong, not paying attention to where you were going, pulling on my leash and yelling, and a big lab came up from behind and scared me to death? D, you must pay attention! There are a lot of things to worry about!

After that incident, whenever you put your running shoes on and get the leash, I go to the bedroom and hide under the bed. I have my interests. Jogging is not one of them.

I hear people say, "Oh, she's just a dog, so it doesn't matter if...she's left alone, doesn't get exercise, doesn't have anyone to play with . . ." you name it. But let me tell you, dogs have feelings, and they are not very different from the feelings humans have. That's the main reason dogs and humans get along so well-in lots of ways, we are alike. Dogs get lonely, sad, scared, and have their likes and dislikes just like humans. Not that you haven't been good to me. Still, a little empathy goes a long way.

By now I was almost eight months old, and M was determined that I get an education. At the time, I didn't see the point. I was already working in the security business and spent a lot of time teaching myself the tricks of that trade. Why should I waste my time in school, I reasoned? M insisted, and made me go back to school. I'm glad she did.

Diary: *September 9, 1992*. Natalie enrolled Rushie in obedience school again. She's older now and more confident around other dogs. She really has a mind of her own, however. Natalie says she's stubborn. Whatever the reason, she doesn't pay much attention to us unless she wants something. In class, Rushie spends more time watching the other dogs than doing her "school work." Natalie thinks she has DADD (Dog Attention Deficit Disorder) and blames me. "If it weren't for DADD," she tells me, "Rushie'd be able to concentrate."

Rushie: Obedience school! Stubborn! Here comes that double standard again. M&D pretty much do what they want when they want. Most of the time when M calls D he doesn't come, either. And M is usually "busy" when D calls.

I know my name and come when I'm called if it seems important. It's not that I don't understand it's just that often I'm busy with other things like guarding the house and don't want to be interrupted. And, if I do agree to come, I think there should be a good reason, like a treat or a ride in the car. The same goes for sitting and staying. Give me a reason! Show me the treats! Besides, being obedient is not that interesting.

Still, I enjoyed obedience school much more the second time. The first thing I noticed when I went into the room was that the dogs weren't as big as I had remembered. More important, all of the dogs were on leashes. I've learned since the first class that if another dog is on a leash or behind a fence, I don't have to worry.

Getting to meet a bunch of new dogs and not having to worry about them biting me was actually kind of fun. There must have been ten dogs in my class-all sizes and breeds. I love to smell them, but I don't like it when they smell me. It's undignified.

One thing I didn't like about the class was the trainer. I call him "Mr. Wolfman." He was such a weird guy. He looked like a wolf dressed as a man or a man becoming a wolf. He had big, bushy eyebrows, and hair growing out of his ears and escaping from beneath the neck of his tee shirt. He always used me for an example. He'd say, "Natalie, bring Rushie up here to demonstrate." At first, I felt good that he used me to show the other dogs what to do. Then I realized that he really wasn't interested in me-he just wanted an excuse to talk to M. One day she wore tight jeans and a tank top. I demonstrated the whole evening! He even grabbed M's hand to "teach" her how to hold the leash! Then he made me follow as they walked around the room. I did what he wanted and when we stopped, he said, "Good Rushie! Good Girl!" He stooped down to give me a treat, which I refused. When he tried to pat my head I backed away. I'll follow if I must, but I did not want Mr. Wolfman touching me.

During class we practiced obedience skills. We learned things like sit, come, and stay. Easy. Before we went home we were tested on what we learned. At the end of one session, all of the owners were in a line with their dogs sitting beside them. Then M took me out in front of the line where everyone could see me and told me to lie down. Then she backed away, telling me to stay. That's pretty hard to do, especially when all those other dogs are sitting around watching. Plus, I felt pretty vulnerable when she was so far away. I think she sensed my concern so she kept repeating loudly, "Rushie stay!" "Rushie stay!" I did.

In fact, I learned everything they taught me
pretty quickly. I also learned that I was a
lot smarter than the other dogs.

Diary: *November 12, 1992.* Well, Rushie passed obedience school
and has a certificate to prove it. Good thing because otherwise we
wouldn't know she attended the class. The trainer said she had
"dominance issues." I don't think it's so much dominance as will-
fulness. She wants to do what she wants to do, period. Talk about
spoiled!

Rushie: D! I can't believe you wrote that.
"Dominance issues!" I think Mr. Wolfman has
the dominance issues. He believed that dogs
should be totally subservient to their "mas-
ters." He even said, "Your dog should think of
you as a god." Can you believe it? A god!

We had a final exam and I performed flawlessly
(well, almost). I only messed up on one part.
It's really hard to concentrate with all those
dogs watching. Besides, you will just have to
get used to the fact that I have my own ideas
about things. If you want obedience, get a
border collie like the one that showed off in
my class.

I learned to sit, lie down, stay, come, heel,
and shake. Not bad, if I say so myself. What I
don't understand is that once I've learned a
trick, why do I have to keep practicing. You
know I can come when I'm called, so why keep
calling me? Do you think I'll forget? Well, I
won't. I can remember all kinds of things:
when it's time for dinner, when it's time to
play, when it's time for a treat. When we ride

in the car, I always know where we are and where we are going.

When you were young and learned your multiplication tables did your mother keep asking you to recite them? No. Once she knew you knew, she quit asking. But you guys never quit.

As smart as I thought I was, at eight months I didn't know very much. My first exposure to life beyond Spokane was when we took a week-long trip to Portland and visited the Oregon coast.

Diary: *November 23, 1992*. We took Rushie on her first road trip last week. We stayed with my mother in Portland for a day and with my brother, Ron, for a few more days before the whole family spent a week at Manzanita Beach on the Oregon coast.

Everything is new and exciting to Rushie. She had a great time driving to Portland and liked staying at my mother's house the first night.

Mom's husband, Lynn, wasn't that thrilled with Rushie, however. His rule is that dogs belong outside–never in the house. As a result of Lynn's attitude and Rushie's mistake (she pooped in the house), we thought it best to stay the other nights at my brother's house.

When we finally left for the coast, Rushie got into her newly discovered "driving position," with her rear legs on the back seat and her front legs on the console between the front seats. From that position she could see where we were going and watched intently.

When we got to the beach house, she was ecstatic, and once inside explored every nook and cranny. Midway through unloading the car, Natalie called Rushie after she took the cooler from the car to the kitchen. No response. Afraid she'd gotten out while we were unpacking, Natalie and I hurried outside and began looking for her. She was nowhere to be found. I thought she might be lost; Natalie was sure a car had hit her. As we were about to split up and search a broader area, mom came to the door and said that Rushie was inside. Apparently she had been going room to room the entire time and when she finished she came to the living room to join the family.

Natalie and I were relieved. It had never occurred to us that Rushie would be so interested in examining the house that she'd spend half an hour on task. When we gathered in the living room, this time with Rushie, we were all commenting about the spectacular view of the sand dunes and waves. Then, Natalie noticed that Rushie was standing next to us, paws on the windowsill, looking out toward the ocean, apparently appreciating the view just like we were. We all chuckled at the sight.

The next day I took Rushie with me for a jog on the beach. Was that ever a mistake!

When I let her off the leash (thinking she'd have more fun running free), a couple of dogs came up and began chasing her. She took off at full speed and ran along the sand until she was out of sight. I finally found her huddled, wet and shaking, behind some rocks in six inches of cold ocean water.

When she saw me she looked relieved. I picked her up and carried her all the way back to the beach house.

Rushie: That was a wonderful trip! I saw so many new things and learned so much. It was the first time I had been to Portland to visit D's mom and brother and the first time I'd gone to the beach. Everything was new and exciting.

When we got into the car, I knew we were going somewhere interesting because M&D had packed lots of stuff in the back. I've learned that usually means we are going on a long trip, not just to the store and back.

I got on M's lap when we left. I stayed there for a while looking out the window, watching all the familiar sights. Pretty soon I didn't recognize anything. Even the smells were different than I was used to. I was starting to get uncomfortable sitting there, but I didn't want to lie down because I was afraid I'd miss something. After a while M put me in the back seat. I thought that was pretty rude and immediately stood up between the seats with my front feet on the center console. I was about to jump back into M's lap when I realized that this was the perfect driving position. I was right between M&D and had a full view of the road ahead. I could check on M and make sure D was driving correctly. Ever since, whenever I get into a car the first thing I do is to get into driving position.

We drove and drove, and I stayed in position for hours looking at the scenery and memorizing the sights and smells.

We finally got to Portland and stopped at Grandma Evans' house. As soon as we went inside I wanted to look around. The house (M later told me it was a townhouse) was small, but nice. Everyone seemed to be happy to see me, but Laura's husband, Lynn, didn't try to pet me and followed me around the house as I explored. He seemed a bit weird, but I didn't pay much attention. (I don't waste my time on people who don't appreciate me.)

While we were in Portland, M took me for walks and drove me around town. I learned where D's brother Ron lives and how to get from his house to Grandma's house. We walked along the river near downtown Portland, and I learned how to get from there to Ron's and Grandma's houses.

The third morning we got up early and M&D put all of their stuff into the car, I got into driving position, and we headed for the beach. D took a road that had a view of the ocean—what a sight! I got so excited I wanted to stop and see it up close. Finally, D stopped the car, M put me on the leash, and we got out. The smells were incredible: salt, sand, seagulls, fish, trees, grass all blended together. I was so excited I tingled all over. As we began walking down a path that led to the beach, the solid ground gradually turned to sand. I'd never felt anything like it before. The sand squished between my toes and flew up when I walked. I hit my feet down hard just to make the sand fly, and then bit the air to catch the grains in my mouth. When we got to the beach D let me off the leash and I ran around in circles chasing the sand. It was so much fun. Then we walked down to the water. The waves were really big, and the water was cold, but I waded in it anyway. I drank the water and discovered that it was really salty. This is where the salty smell comes from, I thought.

After playing in the waves and drinking the salty ocean water for over an hour, I got back in the car with M&D. Soon, I got really thirsty. I kept nudging M, hoping she would give me some of her water. Finally she understood. She poured water into a cup. I couldn't believe how thirsty I was. I drank three cups of water.

Finally, I was able to relax and look out the window. Then after, oh, two minutes I had to pee. I thought I could hold it, but we kept driving and driving. I started to nudge M to let her know I had to go. She didn't get it. I felt like I was going to burst. Frantic, I got on M's lap and pawed on the window. D said, "I think she has to go to the bathroom." Duh. What do you think I've been trying to tell you for the last ten minutes? He pulled the car to the side of the road, and M opened the door. I jumped out before she could put my leash on, which caused her to freak out like she had at the supermarket parking lot. She didn't have to worry. As soon as I hit the ground I started peeing...and...peeing...and....

Finally I got back into the car and we continued our drive. But now I was much more comfortable-pretty much back to normal.

After a while we got off the highway and followed some smaller roads to a big house. When D stopped the car and we got out my first thought was to see what the inside of the house was like. I carefully examined each room, looking out the windows, seeing how the furniture was arranged, and checking all of the smells. I could tell that there had been dogs in the house before, but the odor was faint, which meant that it had been a long time since a dog had stayed there, and that the house had been cleaned.

As I was examining the upstairs rooms, I heard M&D outside calling me. I thought that was strange, since I was inside. I didn't pay much attention because I was busy. When I finished I went to the living room to join the family and see the view. Grandma and Ron were sitting there and seemed really happy to see me. At the time I thought they were overreacting. Then M&D came in and asked me where I had been. Well, I had been exploring the house, I thought. Where had they been?

The next morning D got up early and put his running shoes on. I started to get a little nervous, thinking that he might want to take me with him. Sure enough, he put me on the leash, walked to the beach and started to jog. (By this time I had already decided I didn't like to jog, so I was pretty upset.)

There were lots of people and dogs on the beach, and the dogs especially made me nervous. Remember I'm still young, and haven't been around many dogs, and this was my first time at the beach. As we jogged I worried about how far we were getting from our house and how big the beach was. I hoped that we wouldn't get lost or attacked by one of those dogs.

All of these thoughts were going through my head and I was getting more and more nervous when D stopped and let me off the leash. Then he started jogging again. I thought that he might be trying to run away from me so I tried to stay close. After a while I decided to go back to the beach house. Just as I turned around a big black lab came running toward me. He wasn't on a leash and I couldn't see his owner. I started to run toward D and away from the lab, when two more dogs-neither of them on a leash-came up and started to chase me. I panicked and ran past D down the beach.

I could hear D calling me, but I knew that if I stopped the dogs would catch me. I kept running and running. Finally the sand ended and there were only rocks and water. I continued to run until the water was up to my stomach. I stopped and turned around. The dogs were gone. I couldn't see D. So I just stayed there hidden behind some rocks as the cold ocean water washed over me. I was scared and miserable. I was mad at D for letting those dogs chase me and wondered if I would ever see M again. Just then D came running up. Boy was I happy to see him! As he leaned down to pick me up he whispered in my ear, "I'm sorry I scared you, Rushie, I won't do that again." I wasn't mad anymore.

He carried me all the way back to the beach house and told me how sorry he was. On the way the lab came up to me again. D shooed him away. When we got back M wrapped me in a towel to dry me off and warm me up. Soon I felt better, but I had learned my lesson-I would never jog with D again.

This is when I discovered **Rushie Rule 3**: *Never*

do anything that you know is wrong. Sometimes, people you like or even love will try to get you do something that you know in your heart is wrong. Don't be tempted! Part of growing up is developing a clear and honest understanding of right and wrong. Once you've developed that understanding, don't stray from it. Don't go jogging when you know it's wrong. Don't gulp your food, and never trust a lab.

Part of raising a dog is accepting her individuality. Breeds have certain traits. M&D wanted a fox terrier because of their independent spirit and stunning good looks. M always appreciated my beauty.

Diary: *September 27, 1992.* Natalie was devastated. She took her perfect little Rushie to get clipped yesterday at Wyre Crest Kennels, and the breeder said that, according to the standards of the breed, her legs were too long and her eyes too big. Plus her left ear reaches for the sky rather than bending over as it is supposed to.

We knew about the ear. When we first got Rushie, both of her ears flopped over. When she was about five months old the left one began sticking up. The breeder gave us some glue to hold it down. That worked for a couple of months; then her ear popped up again. After that nothing would hold it down.

Natalie adjusted to the sprightly ear, but to learn that Rushie had two more flaws was like someone telling her that her only child was ugly. Don't worry, Rushie, we love you anyway.

Rushie: Love me anyway! You make it sound like I'm deformed. Actually, I gave a lot of thought to how my ears look. I tried the flop look and it wasn't me-just too casual. I decided that holding the left ear up made me look more alert. Plus, it gives me a distinctive appearance, and I have never aspired to the ordinary.

As for the long legs and big eyes, what top model has short legs and small eyes? The problem with dog breeders is that they believe the best dogs are the ones that embody the average traits of the breed most completely. Well, I am not an average fox terrier, much less an average dog. I am proud to stand out from the crowd. I'm like the model on the cover of *Vogue*: beautiful and distinctive.

About this time, I got my first exposure to water—deep water.

Diary: *September 2, 1992.* We've discovered another of Rushie's fears—she is afraid of, yet strangely fascinated by, water. When Rushie was six months old, Natalie accidentally squirted her with the hose when she got too close to the flowers she was watering. Instead of jumping back, Rushie immediately decided that it was great fun to get doused by the hose, to the point that we now have to lock her in the house when we water the flowers or wash the car. She displays equal fascination with sprinklers. Yet, as much as she loves water from sprinklers or hoses, she always shies away from deep water and swims only when she has no other choice.

Last weekend, she had her first "swimming" experience. We took a hike up to 2 Mouths Lake in Northern Idaho, and she fell in. She didn't like that one bit.

Rushie: I've always liked water. I love to play in the spray from the hose. It's so refreshing on a hot summer day. And there's nothing more enjoyable than biting a sprinkler and feeling the water spray inside my mouth. I was never afraid of water, only of drowning. As a puppy I fell in the water a couple of times. At that lake in Idaho, my whole head went under and I couldn't breathe. It was pretty traumatic.

I'm not like some of those dogs who never learn. I try to pay attention to what I'm doing and learn from my experience. If I do something and it seems dangerous, I don't do it again. My motto is "better safe than sorry." I get this from my career in the security business. A good security chief is cautious and suspicious and notices everything.

Sorry. I got off track. I was talking about the time I fell in the water. You know how rambunctious and sometimes careless puppies are? I was like that, too. I was running along the lakeshore, my feet splashing in the water, birds flying, and the grass brushing my nose. The faster I ran, the more I could hear and smell and the less I could see. I was going really fast and took this giant leap and landed right in a deep pool of water. My nose went under. My feet couldn't touch. I couldn't breathe. Finally, I got my head above water and tried to climb out, but I couldn't get my feet on solid ground. Every time I tried to climb up the side I'd fall back, my head would go under and I'd get water up my nose. I tried and tried and just couldn't climb out.

I thought I was going to drown for sure. I began to panic. Just when I had almost given up hope, D came up, grabbed me by the collar, and pulled me out. I was so relieved. That wasn't the only time D pulled me out of a tight spot.

I didn't have as much common sense then as I have now. Pretty soon I was running along the shore again, not thinking about what I was doing or looking where I was going and-you guessed it-I ran headfirst into another water hole. My head went under again, I got another mouthful of water and started choking. This time I was really frantic. I struggled and struggled and finally pulled myself out of the water. It wasn't a pretty picture. I was totally wet and had mud up to my elbows. I was shaking from the cold and probably in shock. I felt lucky to be alive.

Then guess what happened? D walked up, took one look, and started laughing! Laughing at me! As if this whole traumatic experience was funny. To tell you the truth, I don't much appreciate D's sense of humor, and I gave him an indignant bark. After that I thought the best thing to do was to stay on the high ground and see the sights and smell the smells and not even go near the water. I had learned to stay away from the water the hard way-by almost drowning, twice.

In this next entry, D finally acknowledges some of my good qualities.

Diary: *February 13, 2003*. As much as I make fun of Rushie's idiosyncrasies, she has been an incredibly positive addition to our lives. It's hard to describe how much we love her. And although she is not the most affectionate dog in the world, you can tell that she loves us.

I travel a fair amount for work. Rushie loves to ride to the airport and drop me off. It's almost as if she gets a vicarious pleasure from my trip. "Have a good trip, dad. Be safe. I'll see you in a few days," she seems to say as I give her a hug goodbye. When Natalie picks me up on my return, she always brings Rushie, who waits for me eagerly in the car. She greets me and seems to say, "It's so good to have you home! I hope you had a good trip. Mom and I were fine while you were away, but we're so glad to have you back!" Rushie's greeting makes coming home even more special.

Rushie: I like to travel. I've never flown, but I've been to many airports and seen and heard the planes. Airports are exciting places. Cars and people are coming and going. Jet engines roar as airplanes take off and land.

I take D to the airport every two or three months and have since I was a puppy. I get excited when we turn off the freeway and onto the road that leads to the airport. I look for the planes as they land and take off. We pull up to the curb in front of the terminal and D gets out, gets his bag from the back, and gives M a hug. I wait, hoping he won't forget to say goodbye to me. He never does. He gives me a hug and I nuzzle his ear. Then he's gone, and M and I go back home.

For the next few days—sometimes a week—M and I spend quality time together. I really enjoy our time alone. Then, usually when I'm not expecting it, M will say, "Rushie, let's go get Daddy!" That's music to my ears. I run to the door ready to jump in the car. We drive to the airport and pull up to the curb in front of the terminal. If D isn't already there waiting, I keep my eyes glued to the exits so that

I see him as soon as he walks out.

When I finally see him he is always smiling and says hello as he opens the rear hatch to put his suitcase in the car. I hop over the seats to greet him and he gives me a big hug. When he gets behind the steering wheel I sit on his lap and listen as he tells M and me about his trip. When we get home I think how nice it is to have the whole family together again.

The fact that I'm not as demonstrative with my affection as M would like does not mean that I don't care. We all show our affection in different ways, as this next entry illustrates.

Diary: *March 5, 1993*. Natalie treats Rushie just like an overly protective mother would a child. She always keeps her on a leash and is paranoid that she'll run away and get hit by a car. When we go out for the evening, she can't wait to get back home to make sure Rushie's okay. The few times we've gone for several days and left Rushie with a dog sitter or at the (nice and unbelievably expensive) kennel, she's spent much of her time thinking and talking about her "Peewee Puppin."

She even told me that she wakes up every night and leans over and puts her hand on Rushie's stomach to make sure she's still breathing. The funny thing is that about half the time Natalie does this Rushie growls!

Rushie: I love M dearly, but she can be so smothering. When she comes home after being gone for a while she's excited to see me and I'm excited to see her. M and I hang around together a lot. We have our own jobs. She works in her office and I guard the house. We always have lunch together. And when she goes on an errand I usually go with her to keep her company and to make sure she doesn't get lost.

At night I sleep at the foot of the bed. When I was little I slept under the covers with M, but by summer it was just too hot, and now I get under the covers only when it is really cold. M still tries to get me to sleep next to her at the head of the bed, but frankly, I like my space-I like to stretch out and roll over without worrying about hitting someone.

One of the most irritating things M does is to put her hand on my stomach or back in the middle of the night. This always wakes me up and usually interrupts a dream just when it is getting interesting. Not being one to hide my emotions, I growl just to let her know that I am not amused. Knowing why she wakes me in the middle of the night makes me feel a little better. But it does seem a bit much, don't you think?

Besides, at that time of my life I was thinking about other things-like what I saw when I passed a mirror.

Diary: *April 15, 1993*. Rushie likes to watch TV and look at herself in the mirror. On TV she prefers Animal Planet (although she also likes *Seinfeld*). Every time she passes a mirror she takes an admiring look at her reflection.

I tried to get her to recognize herself in the mirror by sitting behind her and waving. That seemed to intrigue her. She turned her head, alternately looking directly at me then at my reflection in the mirror. I think it dawned on her that the mirror was reflecting what was in the room, not just a TV-like image. From then on she paid more attention to mirrors–glancing at her reflection as she passed or sitting in front of a mirror and looking at me, as if to say, "See how smart I am? I can see you in the mirror."

Rushie: TV can be entertaining and it's educational. Cartoons of dogs and cats running and playing are hilarious. The best thing is that watching TV improves my vocabulary. I didn't realize it at first, but over the years my vocabulary just kept getting bigger and bigger. I think watching TV was responsible for a lot of that improvement.

I love to look at myself in the mirror. In fact, understanding how a mirror works was a turning point in my life. At first I thought my reflection was another dog. One time when I was very young, I walked into the bedroom past the mirror and noticed another dog on my right. It startled me at first, and I growled and barked at the image. As I looked more closely I saw that it was a very attractive dog-black and white, trim and athletic. After I sniffed the mirror I realized it was like the dogs you see on TV-it wasn't real.

As I grew older I became puzzled because every time I passed a mirror I saw the same attractive dog. One day I was sitting in front of the mirror and D was on the bed behind me. I looked into the mirror and saw D waving at me. I looked back at him and he was still waving. I looked back and forth from the mirror to D and from D to the mirror. I saw the same thing. After I'd played this game with D a few times, I realized that what I saw in the mirror was what was in the room behind me.

One time D and I were looking at each other in the mirror and I saw him come up behind me and pat me on the head. I finally realized (I'm surprised it took so long) that the dog I saw in the mirror was me. "So that's what I look like. Very cute," I thought. I liked how alert I looked with one ear sticking up.

Then one time after I came back from the groomers I walked by the mirror and glanced at my reflection. I was so startled I jumped. I thought another dog had gotten into the house. Then I remembered the reflection was of me. I looked so trim and neat-even prettier than normal. M would always tell me how pretty I looked when she picked me up at the groomers. Now I knew what she was talking about.

After that I began comparing myself with the other dogs I saw in the neighborhood and came to the conclusion that I am just better look-ing than most dogs, not to mention lots of small children. This was a big confidence boost for me and it was then that I began to feel that I was special.

One of the things I've always appreciated about M is that she includes me in her activi-ties. For example, I was a big help when she started her dessert business, Natalie's Cake Company.

Diary: *March 10, 1993.* I've been gaining weight for the last several months and couldn't understand why. I've been exercising dili-gently, but every time I weighed myself I'd be a pound or two heavier. I began eating smaller portions, jogging longer distances, and spending more time in the weight room. I finally got my weight stabilized, but I was ten pounds heavier than I wanted to be. I couldn't figure out what was going on.

I finally connected the dots. Since Natalie started her business, I had been the principal taste tester. Every night I'd try a new chocolate cake or brownie recipe. It finally dawned on me that the extra 2000 calories a night I was eating because of my taste testing might have something to do with my weight gain.

I told Natalie she'd have to rely on Rushie as chief tester from now on.

Rushie: D doesn't know how to control his appetite. I do.

I always help M in the kitchen. She tells me what she is going to make and what the ingredients are. I've learned about a lot of good recipes that way.

When she started her business she needed someone to test the recipes. Because I was around most of the time anyway, I volunteered to be her chief tester. For example, when she makes the batter for a cake, before she puts it in the pan to bake she puts a small amount on a spoon for me a taste. I smell the sample first (sort of like humans do with wine) and then take a taste. If it is good I let her know by licking my lips. After she gets my approval, she then goes ahead and bakes the cake or spreads the frosting.

M's cakes not only taste good they also are attractive. (M and I usually discuss and sometimes brainstorm interesting and unusual ideas for cakes.) Once, she made a birthday cake for a woman named Molly whose birthday was on St. Patrick's Day. The cake had green and white frosting with a Leprechaun emerging from the top. On the cake she wrote, "Happy Molly's Day!" She made a sheet cake for a friend of D's who had received a promotion. It looked like the front page of the *Wall Street Journal*. The headlines acclaimed the person's success.

I've thought about going into the cake business with her, but that would be a full-time job, and who would guard the house? I'd have to hire another dog for that job, and it probably wouldn't be done right. She'll have get by with me helping on a part-time basis.

I thought it was funny that D couldn't figure out why he was getting fat. If he had asked me I would have told him. When I help M I take only small tastes-I don't eat a whole piece of cake or four brownies. And I never have dessert after dinner. A little self-control is a good thing, don't you think?

The importance of self-control became even more evident after another traumatic experience with water when we went to a lake in Northern Idaho. (What's with those Idaho lakes, anyway?)

Diary: *July 23, 1993.* On Saturday, we rented a speedboat at Priest Lake. My brother, Ron, son Freddy, Natalie, Rushie and I spent an enjoyable day on the water. Rushie loved going fast and getting splashed by the water coming over the bow. But when we pulled the boat onto the shore to have a picnic, she wouldn't get out unless she was carried. Jump into the water to get to shore? Swim with Freddy? No way!

Rushie: From the time I fell in the water holes at 2 Mouths Lake until the next summer when we went for a boat ride, I successfully avoided the water. Then one Saturday morning that summer we all got in the car, which I love, and went for a ride. I knew we were going to go somewhere special because M&D put a lot of stuff in the car and Ron and Freddy joined us.

As we drove, everyone was talking and happy and I was excited. I sat in M's lap most of the time, but also sat with Freddy and Ron, just so they wouldn't get their feelings hurt.

After a two-hour drive we finally stopped by a lake. Before long M was putting me into a boat. I learned that a boat sits in the water, but doesn't get wet inside. (Pretty nifty, I thought.) Then D started the engine and we began moving-slowly at first, then faster and faster until we were speeding across the water. M held me in her arms. The air blew in my face and ruffled my fur. There were smells galore. Every once in a while the boat would hit a big wave and the water would splash over us. I loved it!

Before long we started to slow down, and soon the boat was touching the shore. I wanted to get out, but when I looked over the side of the boat all I could see was...water. Everyone was getting out and walking onto the beach. I thought for a minute they were going to leave me behind. Then D picked me up and carried me over the water to the shore. He put me down on a sandy beach. I wasn't on a leash and could run wherever I wanted.

Soon, everyone was in the water. Freddy and D were swimming, and Ron and M were wading. I didn't want to swim but I didn't want to be left out, either. So I walked to the water's edge, got my feet wet and tasted the water. Freddy, standing waist-deep in the lake, tried to coax me in. I walked out a foot or two, maybe up to my knees, and then went back to shore. I had no intention of going in over my head-I already knew how dangerous that was.

The next thing I knew, Freddy walked up to me on the shore, picked me up and started walking into the lake. At first it seemed sort of fun, but as we got deeper and deeper I started to get scared. Freddy just laughed! I kept wiggling and hoping that he'd carry me back to shore. He didn't. My worst fear came true as he lowered me into the water and let go. All I could think of to do was to run as fast as I could to get out. I did that for a few minutes and finally my feet touched the bottom and I scrambled to shore. I couldn't believe my own brother could be so mean. When I looked around everyone was laughing! I didn't think it was one bit funny.

After a while I dried off and had a few snacks. I felt better and began to relax. Then Freddy grabbed me again and carried me back into the lake. I was scared and my heart was pounding, but this time I was prepared: I started running even before he put me in the water. He teased me like that for a long time, and then took me back to shore. I went over to M and she hugged me. I felt better.

I got scared again when D held me over the water and lifted me into the boat. I was afraid that he might drop me and relieved when he didn't. We took another ride on the lake and had more fun. I enjoyed going fast and loved having the water splash in my face, but I decided that day that I would never, ever swim again.

For a long time after that, every time I saw water, I'd make sure that I didn't wade more than ankle deep. (See Rushie Rule 3.)

For a long time I believed I didn't need to swim. I had fun hiking and doing other things.

Diary: *August 12, 1993.* Whenever we are on a hike and away from traffic I let Rushie off her leash so she can run freely. But we don't just hike and enjoy the scenery; my responsibility is to throw rocks or sticks for her to chase.

I throw. She chases. But she doesn't just run after the rock–she bounds, leaping high into the air as if she had springs in her legs. If I throw a rock into the deep grass off the trail, I swear she looks more like a kangaroo hopping across the hillside than a dog running. Although she sometimes finds the rock, she never brings it to me like a normal dog. Instead, she stops about five feet away and either starts chewing on it (which Natalie hates) or drops it and waits for another throw. I'm not sure why we've never been able to teach her to fetch; it may just be her way of telling me that she's her own dog.

Rushie: Chasing rocks and sticks as we hike is a derivative of the ring toy game. I taught it to D one weekend when we were on the Coeur d'Alene hike.

D accidentally kicked a rock. I immediately chased after it. A few minutes later he kicked another rock, and I chased it, picked it up in my mouth, brought it back and dropped it in front of him. Then I just stood there looking at him, hoping that he would do it again. He understood right away and threw another rock. In a way, this was even more fun than the ring toy game. Because of all the open space D can throw the stick or rock a long way I can run full speed after it. It was really smart of me to invent this game. After that, every time we went for a hike I knew I could look forward to playing our new rock-and-stick game.

I like it best when D throws the stick off the trail into the trees. It gives me a chance to explore. Sometimes when I am off the trail, I have a hard time seeing over the grass and brush, so I jump as high as I can between strides to see better. When I run full speed I can jump high into the air. I love soaring through the air-it's almost like I'm flying.

I have an excellent sense of smell; I would have been an outstanding airport security dog. I also have excellent vision; I could have been a seeing-eye dog as well. I watch where D throws the rock and run after it. When I get close to where it landed I sniff around for a rock that has his scent. I always find it, and every so often I pick the rock up and bring it back to D because I know he likes it. He always tries to get me to "fetch," as if I were a lab or something. I don't do that because the game is about chasing, not fetching.

Not long after I taught D how to throw rocks, Trevor came into the family and I taught him how to behave. I'm a good teacher.

Diary: *September 10, 1993.* We just returned from a weekend in Portland where we introduced Rushie to my brother's new dog, Trevor, a Brittany spaniel about six months old. On the drive down we were excited that Rushie would meet her new "cousin" and have the opportunity to make friends with another dog. At six months, Trevor is already quite a bit bigger than Rushie, but that didn't seem to matter to either of them, certainly not to Rushie.

After sniffing and circling for a few minutes they started to play. Great, we thought, they seemed to be getting along. As they played, running all over the carpet in the living and dining rooms and out onto the lawn in the backyard, Rushie quickly established herself as the leader and Trevor the follower. Ron was devastated.

I learned over the course of the weekend that Ron had never gotten over the fact that his previous dog, Ritchie, also a Brittany male, had been thoroughly intimidated by Tristie. Ron seemed to take Ritchie's failure to prevail personally, as a reflection on his masculinity. Now it was happening again.

Although I laughed at Ron's reaction, I have to admit that I was proud of Rushie and took unseemly satisfaction that my dog had the upper hand over my little brother's bigger dog.

Rushie: I hadn't heard that one about Tristie before, although I've heard a lot about her, God knows. "Tristie was so smart, Tristie was so affectionate, Tristie was so cute." It's sickening. Still, as a breed, fox terriers are superior, so I'm not surprised she dominated Ritchie.

If Ron is so worried about his dog being in charge, why doesn't he get a fox terrier?

I vividly remember the day I met Trevor. After I trained him, he was fun to play with. He's a nice dog and a good friend.

At six months Trevor was bigger than me, but not as strong. I weighed about 18 pounds and Trevor weighed about 25 or 30 pounds and was two or three inches taller than me. Trevor is white with blond markings. His coat is silky and soft, which is nice, but he sheds all over the place. (Terriers don't shed.) He has brown eyes and a nice face.

When I first met him he tried to jump all over me. Well, I put an end to that in a hurry with a growl and a snap. I didn't blame Trevor, after all he was just a puppy. At the time, I thought maybe I was too harsh-I really scared him-but in the long run I think I did the right thing, because from then on he knew I was in charge.

We played for hours that day. We wrestled and ran-Trevor is a fast runner-until we were both exhausted. After we had played in the house for a while, Ron let us into the back yard. He has a nice yard, with lots of room to run. I'd chase Trevor, and then Trevor would chase me. I liked going under the deck, where it is dark and cozy-almost like being underground. Trevor followed me under the deck a few times but then I think he got scared and quit. I like being underground and don't get scared like most dogs.

On that trip I taught Trevor how to play. We pretend to fight. That means we wrestle, roll around the floor, bite softly, and growl and bark. The idea is to have fun. After play fighting for a while, someone has to win, and that is my job. I start to bite a little harder, growl a little louder, and end up with Trevor on his back and me standing with my front paws on his chest. Now Trevor normally plays along, but sometimes he forgets or gets stubborn. That's when I have to be more forceful.

After playing all day, by evening we were both tired and hungry. D and Ron prepared our food and set our dishes down on the breezeway between the house and the garage. Trevor immediately began wolfing his food down. I was dumbfounded. I'd never seen anything like it. While I was still sniffing my food trying to figure out what was in the bowl, he finished his and came over and started eating mine. I watched in dismay as he gulped down all the food in my dish. The next night, D put both of our bowls out like he had the night before. This time I was ready for Trevor. Trevor inhaled his food as usual, while I sniffed, tasted, and took small bites. After he finished, he came over thinking he would treat himself to my dinner like he had the night before. I let him know with a particularly vicious growl that my food was off limits. Then

I took my time finishing my meal, setting a good example, while he looked on.

Ron provides no discipline. Trevor has the run of the house and can cause chaos, particularly when he gets excited. So when I'm in Portland I am the disciplinarian. I make sure that when he is inside the house he stays in the corner or under the table until I give him permission to leave. I keep him off the furniture.

Sometimes M&D get cross with me for making Trevor behave. But I believe that dogs should know their place and that discipline is important. It works. As long as Trevor remembers his place, we get along fine. Every time I go to Portland I look forward to seeing him.

Thinking about this led me to Rushie Rule 4: *When you are right, stubbornness is a virtue.* Don't let others put doubts in your mind. And don't get discouraged if people (or dogs) don't understand. They don't get it and probably never will.

D snow skis every chance he gets. One winter we went to Mt. Spokane and he taught me to ski.

Diary: *November 28, 1993.* I started to ski with my son when he was six years old and living with his mother in Seattle. I bought him ski equipment for Christmas and took him skiing the first time. We had so much fun that I decided to take up skiing myself. Naturally, I wanted to introduce Rushie to the sport as well.

The Friday after Thanksgiving I took Rushie for her first "skiing" experience. My family was visiting for the holiday. The ski areas hadn't opened yet, but Freddy, Ron and I decided to drive up to Mt. Spokane with our skis anyway. Naturally, we took Rushie.

Rushie: I remember that trip like it was yesterday. I was about two years old. Most of the time when I went somewhere it was with M or M&D. It was fun to leave M at home and to go with the boys. I got excited when I realized we were going to Mt. Spokane (M&D had taken me there before in the summer to hike). As soon as I got out of the car I knew that it was going to be a special day because D didn't put me on a leash. When they took out their boots and skis and started walking up the hill, I couldn't figure out what was going on, but I followed hoping it would be interesting. They walked up the hill, and began building a ramp of snow. This was fun because they threw snowballs for me to chase and when they weren't looking I jumped on the ramp and started digging. After digging a few times I quit because I could tell that D was starting to get mad. (Sometimes he has no sense of humor.)

Then D and Freddy carried their ski equipment up the hill above the ramp. They put their boots on, stepped into their skis and began sliding down the hill and over the jump. I raced them down the hill and beat them every time.

One time when we got to the top of the hill D sat down on the backs of his skis. I couldn't figure out what he was doing so I went over to see. When I got close he sat me down on the front of his skis and held me. Then, Freddy came up from behind and gave us a push. We be-

gan to slide down the hill-slowly at first
then faster and faster. We were heading right
toward the jump. Just when I thought we were
going to crash, D swerved around the jump and
we continued down the hill. The snow and
bushes went by in a blur and I could feel the
wind in my face. It was so much fun I barked
and kept barking until we stopped at the bottom of the hill. We walked back to the top and
I skied with Freddy.

I just love skiing!

Life is not all fun and games, as I was learning. By now I was taking my security duties
pretty seriously and learned that it is important to pay attention to detail.

Diary: *December 15, 1993*. Rushie likes to be in control; she lives
by her routines. She gets upset when things are out of place or routines are not followed.

For example, one day Natalie bought a new picture and leaned it up
against the wall, and left it there while she decided where to hang it.
Rushie and I came home later that day. After saying hi to Natalie,
she walked down the hall and saw the picture lying against the wall
about ten feet away. She did a double take, literally turning her head
to one side and back again before stopping to look at the object that
had suddenly appeared. She slowly walked up to the picture and
cautiously looked at it and sniffed. Then she looked back at me as if
to say, "Did you notice that this picture wasn't here before? How did
it get here? Do you expect it to be here long? Please remove it, because it is very much out of place."

Rushie: It was out of place! What you don't
understand is that I am responsible for household security. It's my job. I don't get any

help. It's all up to me. Don't get me wrong. I like my job and believe I make an important contribution to the family, but it "chaps my hide"* when you tease me for doing what I'm supposed to do.

As security chief I pay attention to every detail. If something is out of place I investigate. Every morning I get up, I eat, and I go to work guarding the house. I am on call at any time, day or night, but I am especially watchful during high-risk times in the morning (when the mail carrier and garbage collector come) and in the late afternoon (when people come home from work). I eat lunch with M at noon and then take a nap so I am rested and alert for afternoon guard duty.

I like the house to be in order and to stay that way. Once you have decided on the best place for a mirror, a picture, or a chair leave it there! I also like to be present when things are moved. That way I know that there isn't something suspicious going on.

The time that D refers to was when M brought a picture in the house without telling me. I came home and immediately saw it tilted against the wall. My first thought was that someone had broken into the house. I sniffed the entire area to find suspicious odors. Nothing. I looked behind the picture to see if anyone was hiding there. Nope. Then I looked at M and D to see if they were alarmed. I

---

* An apt phrase I picked up from my brother Freddy.

looked first at them and then at the picture. I wanted to make sure they understood the problem. When I knew they weren't concerned I relaxed. I realized M must have brought it home and was waiting for D to hang it on the wall (which can take a long time, by the way).

This may not seem like a big deal to the average person, but for a security expert like me even small things, like an out-of-place mirror or chair, can be signs of trouble. When I express concern because things are out of place, I am not being silly or cute; I am just doing my job. The household is safer because of it.

In the next entry D writes that I dream in my sleep. He's right. My dreams are important to me and contribute to my mental well-being.

Diary: *January 12, 1994.* As a puppy Rushie woke up at 5:00 AM *every* morning. Now she usually sleeps as late as we do, which is great on the weekends.

Rushie sleeps near the bottom of the bed at our feet, mostly on her side, but sometimes on her back. Her legs always poke straight out like little stilts, and take up as much room as possible for a dog her size.

When Rushie sleeps she dreams. I can't know for sure, but it seems to me that she enjoys her dreams. Usually within a minute or two after she lies down she falls asleep and, within a few minutes after that, begins dreaming. You can tell when she's dreaming because her legs twitch, as if she were running, and she makes happy little chirping sounds. It's really cute. But if her legs are facing me when she's dreaming she kicks me and wakes me up. Sometimes, I turn her over so her legs face Natalie, who doesn't have trouble sleeping. But even in her sleep Rushie is stubborn and usually turns back to her original position after a few minutes. Then, just as I start dozing off again, I feel the beat of those stiff little legs as she begins to run through her field of dreams.

Rushie: I do like to sleep-always have. Although when I was a pup, I had a hard time sleeping through the night, and I'd always wake up early in the morning and try to get someone to play with me. That's when M invented the morning games.

As soon as M gets up she lets me out to go to the bathroom. While I'm outside she hides snacks in the bedroom. As soon as I finish I run back into the house and head for the bedroom. (Sometimes I'm so hungry that I hate to take time to go to the bathroom-I go outside and immediately come back in. That doesn't work too often because M somehow knows whether or not I've done my business.) What better way to start the day than to find four or five treats?

As much fun as morning can be, so is night, but in a different way. I always get a treat to take to bed. I usually go to bed with D. He reads while I snack on a rawhide chew or a pig's ear. It's our time to bond-we don't talk much we just enjoy each other's company.

After I've finished my treat D puts his book on the nightstand, turns the light off, and we both close our eyes. I usually go to sleep right away. Sometimes I wake up and realize that D hasn't gone to sleep yet. I think D worries too much about work and it keeps him awake.

I don't remember exactly when I started dreaming, but I was pretty young, maybe a year old. Since then whenever I sleep I dream. I always remember my dreams, and look forward to nighttime, because my dreams are so interesting.

I have a favorite dream.

I dream that I am running through a big field. There are other dogs with me, but I am way out in front. As I run I can smell the sweetness of the flowers and pungent odor of the grass and the wet earth. I am running so fast I'm almost flying; my feet are barely touching the ground. As I run, birds fly to get out of my way and rabbits hop madly hoping I won't chase them.

My running is effortless. I'm hardly panting. The dogs that are following me are breathing hard and pleading for me to slow down. I keep running. Everyone is saying, "Look at Rushie. She's so fast and graceful. I wish I could run like that!"

Then off in the distance I see water. As I get closer I see that it is a lake. I run to the shore and far across the lake I see M&D smiling and calling to me. I'm no longer afraid of the water, and without hesitation I jump into the lake and begin swimming as fast as I can. I swim so fast that I push a wall of water in front of me with a wake so big that it makes waves on the shore. I love the feeling of the cool water rushing over my body as I swim.

I look back to see what happened to the other dogs. Most of them are just standing on the shore afraid to jump in. A couple of labs, liking water as they do, are swimming but they can't keep up.

I finally reach the other side. M&D are waiting and happy to see me. M tells me how pretty I am and D how strong. They give me treats and scratch my back. Gradually, the other dogs begin to arrive. They are exhausted from the run and the swim. They all sit in a circle around me. After they catch their breath they ask how I can run and swim so fast.

Before I have a chance to answer I hear D asking if I want to go for a ride in the car. He opens the door and I jump in. I get in driving position and he asks me where I want to go. I tell him, and off we go, leaving the other dogs behind, envious.

I've always believed I'm special, and my dream proves it. I'm not afraid of anything, even water, and dogs recognize me as their leader. Because of my dream, I awake every morning confident and ready for the day. I think that if D could dream like I do he would sleep better at night and do his job better during the day.

The next entry is very sad. Big Red and I had developed a strong friendship over the years. One day, quite suddenly, he stopped playing. Eventually, I settled for taking naps with him in the afternoon. After a while, he began to have a strange smell. I didn't know what it was, but I knew it wasn't normal. Not long after that he disappeared.

Dairy: *September 12, 1994.* Natalie took Big Red to the vet this afternoon and had him put to sleep. He was very sick with complications from diabetes. Natalie held him while the vet prepared the injection. He looked up at Natalie and meowed quietly just before he died. Natalie cried at the vet's and cried again when she told me the story that evening. I cried as I listened to her. I wonder how Rushie will take not having Red around.

Rushie: I never knew exactly what happened to Big Red until now. Red hadn't been feeling very well for several months. I could tell that he was too sick to play, so I left him alone. I checked on him three or four times a day and I'd lie down with him to take a nap in the afternoon. I tried to make him feel better, but it didn't seem to help. Toward the end all he wanted to do was sleep. His shiny red fur became dull and matted.

One day M took him with her in the car and left me home. I was jealous. Why did Big Red get to ride in the car when I had to stay home? He didn't even like riding in the car. When M came home Red wasn't with her. M didn't tell me where they had gone, but I could smell the vet on her. Not good, I thought.

M&D were pretty quiet that night. D didn't even throw the toy for me. I couldn't figure out what happened. M told me that Big Red wasn't coming home, but didn't say why. In a way it makes me feel better knowing that he died because in the back of my mind I always wondered if by chasing and jumping on him when

I knew he didn't want to play I had driven him away.

Big Red and I were good friends; he was like a big brother to me. We played all the time. We'd wrestle and roll around on the floor. Almost every afternoon we'd take a nap together. And Red would always join M&D and me on the bed at night.

I learned a lot from Big Red. I learned the importance of being true to yourself and of not always trying to please someone. I learned the value of self-reliance. Too many dogs can't think for themselves and are lost when they're not around humans. And I learned the importance of dignity. Big Red was dignified. He didn't gulp his food. He always kept his composure. I try to do the same. I miss him.

BOOK TWO

THE MIDDLE YEARS: FRESNO, SWIMMING AND THE CABIN-IN-THE-WOODS

Book Two is about my life from when I was
about two and a half and we moved to Fresno
until I was eleven and about to move again.
This book, in other words, covers most of my
adult life. I describe our life in Fresno and
how I became an expert in security and navigation. I relate the wonders of the Sierra Ne-
vada and our cabin-in-the-woods retreat. I describe my harrowing experiences with cars and
wolves and how, in mid-life, swimming became
my favorite summer activity. Book One was
about growing up. Book Two is about how I
chose to live my life.

Diary: *October 25, 1994*. Tomorrow our family will be together again, and I'm so excited. The last two months have been chaotic—I haven't even had time to write in my journal. After six years as dean at Eastern Washington University, I was appointed dean of the Craig School of Business at California State University, Fresno. I've been living in an apartment near campus, while Natalie remains in Spokane preparing for the move.

Deciding to take this job was difficult for both of us. After several years of making specialty cakes, Natalie had an opportunity to buy a small but successful dessert business and was looking forward to the challenge. I had been working with the architects on a new building in Spokane to house the business program. Taking the Fresno job meant I would miss the opening. And we both would miss the many friends we had made in Spokane.

Fresno State's business school recently had received a generous endowment from Sid and Jenny Craig, of Jenny Craig Weight Loss fame, and the endowment would provide the resources to develop an exceptional business program. We concluded it was just too good an opportunity to pass up.

The move was difficult for everyone, but especially for Rushie. She was at her wits' end, especially when the movers took the furniture from the house. Natalie also said that it was clear Rushie didn't tolerate heat very well. What can you expect from a Spokane native? I wonder how she will do in the summer in Fresno, when the temperature regularly soars to triple digits.

Rushie: Everything was different when we moved to Fresno. It started out different when D went on a trip and never came back. At first I thought it was just another business trip-usually he's gone for a couple of days, but sometimes as long as a week. This time, I kept waiting for him to come home, but he never did. Sometimes he'd call, and M would let me talk to him on the phone. I could hear his voice, but couldn't see or smell him. It was weird.

Then Grandma West came to visit. That was pretty exciting. At the time I didn't think too much about it, but it seemed a bit odd that Grandpa West wasn't with her. It also seemed odd that we didn't go to the lake or the park or downtown or someplace like we usually do when we have visitors. Instead, we stayed home, and M and Grandma kept putting things in boxes.

A couple of days later a big truck came to our house and the driver parked it in the driveway. This is contrary to all security protocol, and I quickly went from a Level One Alert to a Level Four Alert, trying my best to scare them away. Instead of thanking me, M put me in the laundry room and shut the door. Then the two men began stealing the furniture. Piece-by-piece, they took it out of my house and put it into their truck.

There I sat locked in the laundry room listening to two strangers loot my house. I was frantic. Why would M lock me in the room and not let me out to stop these criminals? She didn't seem to mind, and I could hear her talking pleasantly with the men who were taking our stuff. Had she lost her mind? I felt guilty and frustrated that I had been unable to stop this travesty. What good am I as chief of security if I let this happen?

By the end of the day almost everything was out of the house. Even my favorite couch in the den was gone. I had no place to rest and no way to guard the house. The next morning, the men in the truck came back and took all the remaining furniture. M and Grandma put their suitcases and the few remaining boxes into the car. The house was completely empty.

When we got into the car I knew that we were going for a long ride. I tried to forget about what had happened to our house.

We drove and drove. At first, I thought we were going to Grandma Evans' house in Portland, but we never turned off on her road. After that I didn't know where we were and didn't have a clue where we were going. I wasn't worried, though, because M and Grandma were laughing and talking and having a good time. We finally stopped driving and got a room in a motel. I'd stayed in a few motels before and this was a nice one. The room had lots of space and smelled fresh and clean. There were interesting places to walk, and M took me on a long walk, which felt good after riding in the car all day.

We were on the road early the next morning. As we drove, I noticed that it was getting hotter and hotter. In the afternoon, the sun shone in the window and made my bed too hot to sleep in. I tried lying on Grandma's lap in the front seat, and that was too hot. Finally, I got on M's lap and put my head in front of the air conditioning vent. In Spokane it sometimes got too hot, but even on the hottest day I could always find a spot to cool off. This was hotter than anything I'd ever felt before, and there was no place to cool off.

When we stopped driving that night and got out of the car, it was like walking into an oven! I couldn't believe it. My feet burned when I stepped on the pavement. I went into the motel room and looked around. It was okay, but had an odd, dusty smell. And there was a bug that made a chirping sound. I tried to catch it, but I couldn't and finally gave up.

After it started getting dark, M took me out for a walk. In Spokane, when the sun sets it cools off, no matter how hot it was during the day. But it didn't cool off here, and after we had walked around for a short time, I took M back to the motel room.

The next morning, we got up early and drove

most of the day. We finally stopped at what I thought was another motel. We got out of the car, and I noticed that it was just about as hot as it had been the night before. M kept saying that D was here. I looked around, but couldn't see him.

We walked up to the door and M knocked. A man opened the door and it was D! I couldn't believe it. We drove for two days and when we finally stopped D was there! What are the odds?

I hadn't seen him for a long time and was really excited. I jumped up on him and licked his face. He rubbed my ears and gave me a big kiss. He was glad to see me, too. When he put me down, I immediately explored each room in the apartment to see what it was like. Sure enough, there were some of our things, and D's smell was all over. I thought it would be fun to stay here for a few days before we went home. I was pretty sure that when we went home, the furniture would be back in the house. I still couldn't believe M would let two strangers take all our stuff.

Little did I know then that I would never see Spokane again. Fresno was my new home.

Diary: *November 30, 1994.* Rushie has adapted to apartment life easily. I think she likes having the family close. Natalie, on the other hand, can't wait to get her own home–apartment life might be okay for graduate students or couples just starting out, she told me, but at this stage of our lives we need a house–and soon! She's taken it upon herself to make sure that we don't stay in an apartment any longer than absolutely necessary.

In addition to becoming personal friends with our realtor and talking to her on a daily basis, Natalie scans the newspaper each morning and drives around the neighborhoods every afternoon, Rushie in tow, looking at houses. That's when we discovered Rushie's passion for real estate. Every morning after breakfast Natalie asks Rushie if she'd like to go look at houses. Rushie gets excited and immediately goes to the door. She hops in the car and gets into driving position, watching intently as Natalie combs the neighborhoods.

As soon as the car stops Rushie gets ready to inspect another house. She enjoys going through houses so much, exploring with such intensity and purpose, that we concluded she must have been a real estate agent or an interior decorator in a former life. She even decides which houses she likes and which she doesn't. One time Natalie stopped to look at the model homes in a new housing development. There were five models, and Natalie and Rushie looked at each. After they looked at the last house, they walked back past the models toward the office. Rushie passed up three houses, but insisted on going back through the fourth, where she walked through every room, stopping at the bay window in the living room, getting up on her back legs and looking out to the front yard, street, and houses beyond. When she was finished they walked past the fifth house, through the office, and back to the car. It was clear which house was Rushie's favorite.

Last night, Natalie told me about Rushie's favorite house, which happened to be hers as well. Unfortunately, the price is beyond our budget. Natalie broke the news to Rushie, who hid her disappointment better than Natalie.

Rushie: I don't know about a former life, but I do know that I love looking at houses. When we first moved to Fresno M and I looked at houses almost every day. I'd wake up early and couldn't wait to get going.

Here's what I look for in a house: I first examine the front yard and entryway. It is important that the yard is clean and the entryway inviting. The smell on the inside of the house is also important. Strong pet odors tell me that the house hasn't been maintained properly. One house I went through smelled like a kennel-the owners had obviously neglected their home.

It is critical to be able to see the street and the walkway to the front door from inside the house. This is a security issue because when I'm guarding a house I need to have a clear view of anyone entering from the street. A good view to the back yard also is important. I prefer a fenced back yard; it makes security much easier if visitors-or intruders-must enter from the front. I like a back yard big enough so that I can play catch with D. (A built-in barbeque is also a plus.) I love summer evenings when we have friends over for dinner and D barbeques. I am a good hostess and visit with each guest. I usually eat with the guests rather than having my regular dinner.

I like the master bedroom to be on the first floor because it's easier to hear intruders and if I have to go to the bathroom in the middle of the night I don't have far to walk. I like to have two bedrooms in addition to the master bedroom. It gives me places to go if I need to get away. I like to have the family room next to the kitchen; that way in the evening I can lie on the couch and watch M fix dinner.

M and I generally have the same taste in houses. Unfortunately our taste is expensive. Too bad D doesn't make more money.

Although the apartment we lived in was nice enough, there wasn't much space. The backyard was tiny, and there wasn't enough room to play the ring toy game properly.

Diary: *December 3, 1994.* Rushie and I played the ring toy game every night when we lived in Spokane. She expected the same in Fresno. Living in an apartment with no room to throw the toy is no excuse, as far as Rushie is concerned. Every night after dinner she gets her toy and brings it to me to throw. A couple of nights ago, Natalie and I were in the living room watching TV when, as usual, Rushie brought me her toy, telling me it was time to play. So I grabbed the toy (Rushie always tries to grab it first) and threw it about ten feet to the other side of the room. She eagerly ran after it and brought it back, tossing it in the air and catching it in her mouth several times before dropping it on the floor just out of my reach. She sat down and watched me closely and tried to grab the toy before I could. We did this several times and she seemed to enjoy the game even though the room was small and the throw short. The third time I tossed the toy it hit the vertical blinds covering the sliding glass door to the patio. The blinds rattled and swayed back and forth. Rushie, being the cautious dog she is, froze for a full five seconds and then slowly walked up to the toy now captured by the blinds. One edge of the toy was sticking out from under the blinds. As she got closer she realized that to get her toy she would have to put her nose perilously close to the blinds that had rattled and waved in the air. A scary proposition for sure. She slowly crept up to the toy. Just as she was about to put her mouth on it, I yelled, "Boo!" She jumped at least a foot in the air. Then she looked back at me as if to say, "D. Stop it!" Finally, she got her nose close enough to the blinds to grab the toy and brought it back for me to throw.

I threw the toy two or three more times, the last time into the blinds, causing them to "come alive" once again. She went through the same cautious routine. Just as she got her mouth almost around the toy I yelled, "Boo!" She jumped in the air again. This time she turned around and ran to me jumping up and barking indignantly, as if to say, "D, that's not funny. Stop it!"

Rushie: D is always teasing me. He thinks he's funny. I don't know how many times he's hidden in a doorway and jumped out and yelled. "Boo!" as I went by. Most of the time I know he's there-I either see or smell him. But sometimes he takes me by surprise, and I really jump. I've never understood why this is supposed to be so funny. I think it's just weird.

Every time I go up the stairs ahead of him he tries to pinch my rear. That's supposed to be funny, too. I've gotten to the point that, if I'm on the stairs and he's behind me, I start to run just in case he's thinking about pinching me. Sometimes I outrun him, and when I get to the top of the stairs I turn around and bark, just to let him know I won. Now *that's* funny.

Grabbing D's sock while he's trying to get dressed and running when he chases me is funny. Stealing his napkin while he's eating. That's funny, too. But the funniest thing is when M says, "Rushie! Let's get Dad!" and she starts grabbing and pinching him. I join in with growls and playful bites. D raises his arms and tries to protect himself, but we get him anyway. That's really funny. Actually, I think I have a better sense of humor than D.

Hence, **Rushie Rule 5:** Never lose your sense of humor. I'm not a frivolous dog. I go to work and put my life on the line every day. In my work I see things that would make most individuals bitter and cynical. Every day people, dogs, and the occasional cat try to break into our home. I am the first and last line of defense for the entire family. Sometimes by the end of the day I am exhausted by my encounters. I could curl up in a ball and dwell on them and become bitter and angry. Instead, I happily greet D when he comes home and steal his napkin when he sits down to dinner. Humor helps me put the events of the day into perspective and helps me prepare for the difficult day ahead.

After looking for months, M and I finally settled on a house that we liked and D could afford. It was in a great location, but needed a lot of work.

Diary: *April 2, 1995.* I'm finally getting settled in at the university–there's so much to learn and do the first few months of a new job–and have been going with Natalie, Rushie and the real estate agent to look for houses. We finally found a house right on the water at Woodward Lake. It needs major remodeling, but because it costs less than we anticipated we can afford the work. We moved in a month ago, and the contractors are already tearing down walls. The kitchen is gutted, and we eat on TV trays in the bedroom. I hate the mess and inconvenience, but Natalie and Rushie are into the whole process.

Rushie: M and I looked at 30 or 40 houses before we chose this one. I like the basic layout of the house. It has a back yard that faces the lake. It even has a dock and a boat.

M&D and I have taken the boat around the lake a few times. It's really interesting to see the other houses and to wave at the other boaters.

Whoever built the house knew security. In the front of the house I have a good view of the yard and street from windows in the dining room and den. Every room that faces the back of the house has windows. The back yard is secure, with fences on both sides and the lake in the rear. The only threat from this direction is boaters who sometimes come too close to our property in the evening. Peak guarding hours in the front are morning and late afternoon. In the evening I guard the back of the house while M fixes dinner. I can be where I'm needed throughout the day.

Only a few weeks after we moved in, workers began remodeling the house. I was concerned at first, but felt better after M explained what they were doing and that it would look much better when they finished. I started looking forward to seeing the workers each morning. I especially liked Bryan, who owned the company doing the work. Each morning he'd say hi and ask me how I was doing. I'd follow him around as he worked, and answer any questions he had about the job. Sometimes when I didn't know the answer, he'd tell me to get Natalie. I'd bring her back and the three of us would discuss what should be done.

After Bryan took out the old appliances and removed the counter tops in the kitchen, we ate on TV trays in the bedroom. M&D got tired of that routine pretty quickly, but I thought it was nice. They'd sit on the end of the bed and eat off the trays while they watched TV. I'd lie between them and watch them eat. I didn't even have to move when they offered me a snack. The only thing I didn't like was that M got most of the food from the deli, and it didn't taste as good as when she cooked the dinners herself.

We spent a month eating our dinners from TV trays in the bedroom, and it was three months before the remodeling was done. I think the house looks much better now. They expanded the family room and removed a wall between the kitchen and the living room. I now have easy access to all of the windows that face the back yard. This may seem minor, but in the security business small things add up. The workers also installed a patio cover in the back. Now I can lie outside in the shade and keep an eye on things.

I was disappointed when Bryan quit coming to our house every morning. One time he came back for a visit, and we had a nice chat. I told him that he did a good job on the remodel and that we were all very happy. He took pictures of what he had done so he could show them to other customers.

M&D appreciate me more for my human-like qualities than for my canine qualities. My involvement in the remodel is an example-M discussed all of her ideas with me and we made decisions together. At the same time, they seem surprised when I don't act like a dog or identify with other dogs. Go figure.

Diary: *June 15, 1995*. Rushie is obsessive about other dogs. She's intrigued by the idea of another dog, but intimidated when she actually confronts one. For example, when she's in the car or at her perch in the front window of the house and she sees a dog she goes crazy with vicious growls and loud barks. She acts as if the offending dog (or cat) is her mortal enemy and viciously pledges to fight until the death to defeat it and to protect our home and her honor.

But when she actually confronts another dog face-to-face it's another story. No matter how small the dog, if it moves quickly or in a way that could possibly be interpreted as aggression, she is completely intimidated.

Rushie: I continue to be amazed by how profoundly I am misunderstood by my own family. You would think that being around them night and day, paying attention to their every mood, and sacrificing my desires for theirs, would result in their having a better appreciation for my feelings. Apparently I expect too much. This is but another example of why this autobiography so important.

Let me clarify: I am not afraid; I am cautious. There are lots of crazy dogs out there and more than a few crazy cats. I think it is only prudent to determine the mental stability of the beast before I let my guard down. Once I've determined that the dog isn't rabid or insane, I relax.

This brings me to **Rushie Rule 6**: *Better safe than sorry*. Perhaps it is because I am in the security business, but I believe that caution is a virtue. Spontaneity has its place, but on the big issues in life try to minimize your risks by looking at the evidence carefully and not letting yourself get carried away by emotion.

Under the influence of dog trainers like Mr. Wolfman, many dog owners think that dogs should do whatever their human partners say and be happy about it. Well, that's not how it works. A responsible owner takes her dog's feelings into account. This shouldn't be hard to understand, but apparently it is. Consider the following entry in which D is completely confused about the purpose of walking your dog.

Diary: *July 20, 1995.* Natalie just returned from another frustrating walk with Rushie. Natalie likes to take Rushie for walks. But Rushie is fickle. Some days she's just not interested. Other days she'll go outside and determine that it is too hot, and go back into the house. When she's willing, she has her own routes, and they are not the same each time. She always starts her walks with purpose, as if she has already planned where she is going. And if Natalie wants to go one way and Rushie another, Rushie sits down and refuses to budge until she gets her way. She'd rather go back home than follow someone else. The only time she will consider giving in is when the three of us are walking. Walking with the entire family seems to put her in a more flexible mood.

In walking, as in the rest of her life, it is clear that Rushie has her own agenda, and she is not to be distracted.

Rushie: Let's begin at the beginning. What's the purpose of walking a dog? The purpose is to give her exercise and fresh air and to make her happy, right? Ask any dog owner why they walk their dogs and they'll say, "Because my dog likes it." They don't say, "I walk my dog because I enjoy it and, frankly, I don't care what the dog thinks." That would sound too selfish, even for most humans.

In theory M&D would agree that the purpose of walking a dog is to benefit her. But like many dog owners, they fail to put theory into practice.

M normally takes me on walks. She says it is for my enjoyment, of course. But if that's true, why does she insist on taking me for a walk even when I don't want to go? Why, when we start walking, doesn't she follow me? If it is for my enjoyment, why can't we go home when I want to? It's obvious from what actually happens that walks are more about her than me.

M and I are very close. I listen to her when she talks about all sorts of things and pretend to be interested. I cuddle with her during the day and return her kisses. I ride in the car with her when she goes to the store and wait patiently until she returns. I never fail to say hello when she comes home. When M is sick and stays in bed, I curl up on the corner of the bed to keep her company. Even when I leave to guard the house, I check on her frequently to make sure she's okay. I try to be thoughtful and considerate.

In most ways, M is as thoughtful and considerate of me as I am of her. Consideration flies out the window when it comes to walks, however.

M usually walks in the late afternoon or early evening. The summers in Fresno are really hot, and the one thing I can't tolerate is heat. There were even a few days in the summer in Spokane when it was so hot that all I wanted to do was to lie on the cool tile floor under the staircase. And that was when I was young and hardly anything bothered me. Now that I'm older and more experienced I have pretty definite ideas about what I like and don't like. To be perfectly clear: I don't like heat!

Put yourself in my place. It is a hot summer day in Fresno; the temperature is in the triple digits. Despite the heat I've spent the entire morning in the den guarding the house. By the afternoon it's too hot to bear, and I slowly walk, tongue hanging out, in a desperate attempt to get cool, to a special place in the family room behind the couch where I can lie on the bare wood floor and bask in the flow of cool air from vent overhead. The afternoon sun blazes through the windows reflecting off the lake to the west of the house. Good thing, I think, that I can get behind the couch and block the sun. Between the cool air and the cool floor I finally start to get comfortable.

Then the worst thing I can imagine happens. I see M holding her tennis shoes. I hear her putting them on. I realize she wants to go for a walk, and she'll probably want to take me. Just the thought of going outside in the heat of summer makes me light headed. I scrunch further into the corner, hoping she'll forget about me. No luck. I hear her calling, "Rushie, let's go for a walk!" I try not to move or even breathe. The first time she passes she doesn't see me. Dare I hope? In a cheerful tone that sends shivers down my spine, she calls out, "Rushie! Come. Let's go for a walk. It will be fun!" as she methodically searches room to room. My heart sinks as I see her coming toward me, leash in hand, saying, "Oh, there you are!"

She bends down and I hear the metallic snap of the leash being secured to my collar. I'm trapped and I know it. I reluctantly follow her to the door. I am optimistic. Maybe it isn't as hot as usual today. After all, it would be nice to get outside and stretch my legs. My optimism is dashed as the door opens and I feel the blast of hot air. That's when I decide I'm not going. I turn to go back into the house. The leash pulls me back out. As I resist its pull, I imagine the white-hot pavement scorching my feet. It gives me strength and resolve. I decide right then that there will be no walk for me today. I sit down and refuse to budge. My resolve is rewarded when M takes me back into the cool house and shuts the door. I can tell that she's disappointed, but I don't care. If this walk is for me as she pretends, then it should be my choice whether to go or not. This time I choose not to go.

Attention, dog owners! Please remember that the purpose of walking your dog is to keep her healthy and happy. It follows that you should let her walk where she wants, when she wants.

The dog should lead.

I don't mean to give the wrong impression; most of the time I enjoy my walks. I especially like it when D comes. (I'm family oriented and like it when we do things together.)

When we begin our walks I like to turn left at the end of the driveway and return from the opposite direction. The reason is that there are certain yards and smells I like to investigate right away and others that can wait. There's a black cat two doors up on the other side of the street I like to scare. If I can do this right away it sets a positive tone for the entire walk. The other end of our street is much less interesting, so I leave it until the end of the walk.

When we get to the main road, there are a variety of interesting walks to choose from. Because it's my walk, I strongly believe that the choice should be mine. I don't always choose the same route; it depends on how I feel that day. On days when it's cool and I don't have other appointments I sometimes go back to the apartment we lived in before we bought the house. That walk takes more than an hour, but I enjoy visiting the old neighborhood and seeing how it has changed. If I feel like taking a short walk I choose another route that only takes about 15 minutes. Walking all around the lake takes about 45 minutes. There are six different routes I take regularly and even more that I take occasionally. Each has something I like about it-a particular yard to explore or a dog to see-the walk I choose depends on the weather, my mood, and how much time my schedule allows.

M usually lets me choose the route I want. If she forgets or starts going in the wrong direction I let her know by slowing down and looking in the direction I think we should be headed. If she doesn't get the hint, I stop to sniff something and then start walking in the direction I prefer. If for some reason she still doesn't get it, I just sit down and refuse to move. That always works. D, on the other hand, can be very stubborn. If he starts going the wrong way on a walk, I do my best to let him know. But if he has his mind made up, I usually give in and go along to avoid a scene.

As long as I'm allowed to choose my route and walk at my own pace, I'm fun to be with. To me, stopping periodically to smell the different fragrances and to determine who else has been there recently is crucial for an enjoyable walk. To M, the most important part seems to be whether or I poop. As soon as we start the walk, it's always the same, "Come on, Rushie. Let's go poops and peewee." When I poop, she pulls a plastic bag out of her pocket, reaches down and carefully puts my poop in the bag and carries it all the way back home! (I've never been able to figure out why she has this disgusting obsession. Otherwise, she seems quite normal.) Let me tell you that it's pretty embarrassing to have her talking about bowel movements all the time. I've learned to finish my business as soon as I can to get her to change the subject.

I don't agree that I'm a problem walker like D says. He just can't get over the fact that I don't jog.

On summer nights when it's not too hot, a nice alternative to a walk is to take a boat ride on the lake.

Diary: *July 29, 1995.* On of the best things about our Fresno house is that it backs up to Woodward Lake, where we have a dock and an electric boat. In the summer we cruise around the lake. Rushie loves these rides.

Yesterday we decided to go for a boat ride. As soon as I told Rushie, she got excited and stood on the dock. The boat cover was barely half way off when she hopped aboard. Natalie brought the wine and cheese and I shoved off, with Rushie perched on the seat behind the wheel.

We took our usual route, about fifty feet from shore, and started around the lake. It was a beautiful evening–the sun was setting into a red sky, the air was warm, and the wine was excellent. Rushie was enjoying herself, taking an occasional bite of cheese, and examining each house and yard carefully as we passed.

After a few minutes we passed a house with a black lab in the yard. Rushie began to bark furiously. The dog looked up and ran toward the shore, barking in return. Instead of stopping at the shore, as Rushie expected, he jumped in the water and started swimming rapidly toward the boat.

Rushie's mood instantly changed from aggression to anxiety. "See our brave fox terrier," I said with irony. Natalie laughed at Rushie's sudden anxiety.

Rushie: I didn't think it was all that funny.

Anyway, I wasn't scared. Surprised, maybe, but not scared.

I love riding in our boat. I get to see all of the houses around the lake. Most of the houses are nice and have well-landscaped back yards. A few are not so nice. I like to look at the yards and see what changes and improvements have been made.

When M&D see people they wave. When I see dogs I say hello with a polite bark or two. The time D talks about we were on the lake and passing the back yard of one of those houses that need landscaping. The lawn was brown and what shrubs and flowers there were looked practically dead. It was obvious that a dog had been digging in the yard.

I saw this scruffy dog come out into the back yard. I said hello just to be nice. I could tell from his bark that he was not going to be nice in return. He ran, barking viciously, toward us. Instead of stopping at the water's edge like a normal dog, he jumped in and started swimming toward the boat. That's when I realized he was a lab. (I can't stand labs!) He was catching up to the boat, and I got worried about M&D. I quickly issued a Level Two Alert. My mind raced as the dog swam closer. I knew that I could beat him in a fight, but if he actually got on board, it would be a mess, and M&D might get bitten. I escalated to a level Three Alert.

He was maybe 30 feet from the boat when I went to Level Four. D finally sped up. The dog couldn't swim as fast as our boat was going so he finally gave up. I was relieved, not because I was scared, but because we avoided what could have been an ugly confrontation where M&D could have been hurt.

M&D laughed at me, but I didn't care. We were clear of the danger. It's no picnic being chief of security.

It was then that I discovered **Rushie Rule 7**: *Never, ever trust a lab!* Labs slobber and knock things over and should never be let in the house. When they are outside they should always be on a leash. They are excessive eaters and should only be given dry food. I'm not being harsh. I'm being realistic. Some breeds need special treatment.

On summer weekends when the temperature soared we sometimes drove to the ocean or to the mountains, where it was cooler. I looked forward to those trips.

Diary: *January 13, 1995.* I'm really beginning to like Fresno. We're in the middle of California's Central Valley–the agricultural center of California and the nation. Fresno is also central to all sorts of outdoor activities; there are lakes and reservoirs, mountains and oceans. From my house, it is a little more than a two-hour drive to the central coast and just over an hour to Yosemite National Park. More important, it is less than an hour and a half from my house to Sierra Summit, a local ski area with seven chairs and nearly 2000 feet of vertical drop.

People refer derisively to the snow as "Sierra Cement," but they exaggerate. The snow isn't as light as it is in Utah and Colorado, but it is certainly skiable. And the weather makes up for any lack of snow quality. In the Sierra the weather is either sunny or stormy. There are few foggy or gloomy days. That means good visibility and great skiing conditions.

After two years of driving to Sierra Summit each winter weekend, we started looking for a cabin in the mountains. We find the area near Shaver Lake especially attractive. It takes 45 minutes to drive from my house to Shaver Lake and another 25 minutes or so to get to the ski area.

We are looking for places to buy, with Natalie and Rushie taking the lead.

Rushie: I'd been to the mountains near Fresno several times before we started looking for our own place. One time we spent a weekend with friends at their cabin. A couple of other times we drove up for the day. When M and I began looking at cabins around Shaver Lake, I got really excited because I'd been there enough to know that I wanted to go there more often. One summer we spent almost every weekend in the mountains looking. I loved it! I looked at each cabin carefully and shared my thoughts with M&D.

Eventually we narrowed our search to two choices. One was an older cabin in town and the other was a newer cabin on the outskirts of town. I loved the big rock fireplace in the older cabin, but I could smell where water had leaked inside onto the kitchen floor. That would have to be fixed. There was a nice deck in the front with a view to the street below, but the view from the front window was obstructed, so I could tell it would present a security challenge. The newer house smelled

clean and dry. It had a nice deck that allowed
a clear view of the ravine in back of the
cabin. It had windows on the side and in the
bedroom that I liked for security reasons. It
wasn't quite as big as the older one, but it
was nicer.

M and I liked the newer cabin best, and D finally agreed. I love the cabin, and after we
moved in I remembered how much fun it is to
play in the snow. I think we made a good
choice.

Diary: *April 17, 1995*. We spent the first weekend in our new cabin.
We left Thursday night and came back Sunday. We even had snow
on Friday and Saturday. Not the warm and slushy spring snow you'd
expect, but light powder and cold temperatures typical of a winter
storm. The skiing was fantastic. When I got back to the cabin Friday
afternoon, Rushie greeted me at the door, excited about the snow
and hoping I'd take her out to play. We played for more than an
hour, and when I finally made her come inside she had great gobs of
snow clinging to her fur. We both sat in front of the fire and warmed
up while Natalie fixed dinner. After dinner, we went for a walk. The
falling snow had covered the trees and created an unnatural silence.
The only noise was the crunch of our shoes on the snow and the
snap of Rushie's teeth as she jumped toward the sky trying to catch
snowflakes in her mouth. I watched Natalie smiling and Rushie
playing and knew that our decision to buy the cabin was the right
one.

Rushie: I remember our first weekend at the
cabin. It was heaven.

M&D packed up the car on Thursday when D got
home from work. I couldn't figure out exactly
what was going on. There wasn't enough luggage
for a long trip, but I could tell M&D were ex-

cited and happy, so I thought it might be something special. After we'd been driving for a while I realized we were heading toward the mountains, and I hoped we might spend the weekend there looking at houses. Just before Shaver Lake we turned off the main road, drove for a short way and stopped in front of a cabin we had looked at several times before. We got out and went inside to look around. The place was just as I had remembered-nice living room, with a big fireplace, and a deck that overlooked a ravine. M&D got the luggage out of the car and brought it inside. Great, I thought, we're going to stay overnight.

After dinner we went for a walk. The sky was clear, the air was cold, and I was excited. The fragrance of the pine and cedar trees filled the air. Mixed in was the smell of all sorts of wild animals, which made the walk seem like an adventure. I was struck by how similar the smells were to the ones I remembered when we hiked in the forests near Spokane. I was so happy I started tingling all over, just like I did when I was a puppy. I looked up at M&D, and I could see they were just as excited. With a barely suppressed grin, D said, "Look at all the stars, Natalie. Brilliant, aren't they? And everything smells so clean and fresh." After a pause, M looked first at D then at me and then at me and said, "I think buying the cabin was the right decision, don't you?" "I hope so," replied D. D, cautious as ever, may not have been sure about the decision. But I was. I knew that our cabin-in-the-woods would make our life much more interesting and enjoyable.

The next morning I got up early. It was still dark outside. I tried to wake M&D, but they wouldn't budge, so I took a close look at the cabin. The house wasn't built with security in mind, but with windows on three sides I could at least do my job. No need to worry. As I lay on the sofa in front of the fireplace, I noticed I could see out a window on the side of the house and through the sliding glass door to the deck and ravine beyond. Nice, I thought. In the winters I could relax in front of the fire and still do my job.

M&D finally got up. D went skiing and M and I spent the day deciding what furniture to buy and what remodeling was needed. After lunch, M and I were relaxing on the couch thinking about the best color to paint the walls. I must have dozed off, because the next thing I heard was M saying, "Rushie! Wake Up. It's snowing outside!" I looked out the window and sure enough big snowflakes were falling gently to the ground. I walked to the window to get a closer look and saw that the ground was covered in white. What a delightful surprise.

I looked back at M and saw she was already putting on her coat. She opened the door and we went outside. I looked up and tried to catch the snowflakes in my mouth as they fell to the ground. I ran and jumped and chased—it was the first snow I'd seen since we left Spokane. I was so happy! We took a long walk and by the time we got back we both were covered with snow.

D was beaming that afternoon when he got back from skiing. I knew the skiing had been good. As soon as he changed out of his ski clothes, we went outside and played. He threw snowballs, and I chased them. It's my favorite winter game.

When we went back inside D made a fire in the fireplace. Soon the flames were roaring. D and I sat in front of the fire, warming up after our play. That night M fixed a good dinner-beef stew, French bread, and salad, as I recall. After dinner D asked if I wanted to go for a walk. Absolutely, I said.

It snowed all day Saturday. After D came home from skiing we went outside to play. I chased snowballs, jumped in the snowdrifts, and explored the ravine behind the cabin.

After dinner D asked who wanted to go for a walk. I said I did, but M decided to stay at home by the fire. D put on his heavy jacket and black felt hat. When we walked outside, I thought, perfect, it's still snowing. He lit a cigar (he only does that when M isn't around), and we started walking. I looked up at him and could see he was very happy, maybe the happiest I'd ever seen him. There was a slight smile on his lips, and his black hat was soon white with snow.

I chased the snowballs he threw. After running and chasing for a while, I decided to walk by his side. He looked down at me and said, "Rushie, I think we made the right decision. And I think God agrees. He sent us this wonderful snow for our very first weekend. We're going to love this place."

I knew he was right.

As much as I loved going to the cabin in the winter, I loved going in the summer just as much. Even on the hottest days in Fresno, the air was cool and fresh at the cabin.

Diary: *July 5, 1996.* Like a lot of Northwesterners, Rushie believes that any temperature warmer than 75 degrees is hot. The cabin at Shaver Lake is probably the only thing that makes the hot Fresno summers tolerable for her. Maybe it's because the climate reminds her of Spokane.

Rushie: I love everything about the cabin. I love the cool air, the trees, the smells, and the games D and I play. When we go to there, everyone is in a good mood because we know we are going to have fun. M cooks great meals-stews and chilies in the winter and barbecued steaks and salmon in the summer. In the summer we go on long hikes, and in the winter I chase snowballs. The weather is perfect at the cabin-with cool summers and cold, snowy winters.

M was happy when we moved to Fresno; she thought Spokane was too cold. I remember that she was always complaining about the snow in the winter and the cold nights in the summer. I was born there and I guess I was used to it. I never remember being cold (except for that time M left me for hours in the car while she was shopping).

In Fresno I was hot all the time. In the summer I would lie on the cool wood floor in the family room during the hottest time of the day. I'd try to sleep or at least not move much until it got dark. Then I'd go outside and play the ring toy game with D. I love that game, but some nights in Fresno were so hot that I had to quit after a few tosses. In Spokane, I loved to sunbathe. I tried that in Fresno, but it was too hot.

Fortunately, we went to our place in the mountains often.

There is a ravine behind the cabin that I like to explore. It's full of the most interesting sights and smells. D and I have a special game we play: D stands on the top of the ravine and throws rocks to the bottom. I stand with him at the top and watch where the rocks go, then chase after them as fast as I can. Once I get to the bottom I wander around while I'm looking for the rock. It's a great place for smells. I can smell birds, squirrels, snakes, and occasionally a coyote. D stays at the top of the ravine and watches me. He's always impressed when I find the rock and bring it to him, so I do that every once in a while just to keep him happy. When he quits playing and goes into the house, I sometimes stay in the ravine for a few minutes longer, but without the rocks to chase and D to watch, it gets boring.

In the winter, the snow slides off the roof of the cabin and into the ravine, which becomes steep and slippery. When that happens, D takes

me to the back there and throws snowballs. I
race down the steep, snowy slope. Sometimes I
sink in and fall face first into the snow,
other times, when it's icy, I slide all the
way to the bottom. What I like best is when
the snow is fresh and dry, and I can run down
the slope with the snow spraying up around me.
Sometimes, it is so soft that I feel like I'm
floating. I think it's the same enjoyable
feeling D gets when he skis on fresh powder.

Although I had lots of fun at the cabin, I
also did my job and made sure the proper security protocols were in place.

Diary: *October 27, 1995*. Rushie has a keen sense of responsibility
and dedication to task. Every time we go to the cabin, she makes
sure it is safe. It's almost like she has a checklist of things that must
be done.

Rushie: I am meticulous and systematic about
everything.

I've got the drive to the cabin memorized-I
know every turn and every intersection by
heart. Not to brag, but I know where we are
even if I'm not looking. I count the turns as
we drive and can tell from the smells exactly
where we are at any given time.

When the two-lane road turns into four lanes,
I always look out the window. I like standing
on M's lap so I can watch the road. In the
winter, I get excited when I see snow because
I know I'll get to chase snowballs. At the top
of the four-lane, I get in D's lap and put my
nose next to the open window so I can smell

the fresh air. When we turn onto our street I like to put my whole head outside and savor the smell of the trees and animals.

After D parks the car in front of the cabin, my work begins. I insist on getting out first, and immediately inspect the yard to make sure everything is in place and to determine what animals have been trespassing on my property. Most of the time I smell birds and squirrels and a few snakes. I get concerned when I smell coyotes. Coyotes are vicious wild animals and can't be trusted.

I like to be first in the house, for security reasons. I look to see if anyone drank my water or ate my food. (I check these first not because I am hungry or thirsty, but because I know that if anyone ever broke into the house he would go for the water and food first.)

I walk all around the house searching for intruders and for signs that someone or something had been there while we were gone. When I'm satisfied that everything is okay, I take a break on the couch while D starts the fire.

After the fire is burning I go back outside to double check for dangerous animals. After I secure the front yard I go back inside and directly out onto the deck. I am alert to the scents of dangerous animals and look for any movement in the ravine below. Once the back yard and ravine are secured I come back into the house and relax, knowing the family is safe.

The routine may seem boring or tedious to some, but this is the job of the security chief. And, I don't cut corners.

D is an exercise fanatic, and even though he spends an hour or two every day at the gym, when he gets home he never fails to make sure I get my exercise.

Diary: *December 3, 1995.* I am a believer in exercise. It keeps me healthy, trim, and energetic. Dogs need exercise as much as humans, and I try to make sure Rushie gets her share. Natalie walks her almost every day, and I toss her ring toy almost every night. The combination of walking and chasing her toy keeps her fit and calm (or at least as calm as a fox terrier can be).

Our Fresno house is at the end of a cul de sac, with little traffic. Every night I take Rushie outside and throw the ring toy for her. When I see the headlights of an oncoming car, I stop throwing and call Rushie to me. Simple and safe, or so I thought. Natalie always worries that a car speeding around the corner could hit Rushie, but I knew better. It was a cul de sac, not a thoroughfare, I told her.

A week ago last Tuesday we were playing our usual game in the street. In an instant a car sped around the corner. The driver didn't see Rushie, and Rushie didn't see the car. The car's left front tire hit her and she yipped as she fell to the ground.

I was scared then immensely relieved. The tire had only pinched her right front leg. I picked her up and she literally clung to me. Natalie heard the commotion and ran outside. She panicked when she saw that Rushie had been hit.

We called around and found an animal emergency facility that was open. The vet said that nothing was broken, but that she needed stitches, antibiotics, and dressings on the wounds. After he treated her and we paid $450, we took her home.

By the time we went to bed it was 1:00 a.m. Natalie had been holding Rushie the whole time, and of course, blaming me for the near tragedy. I was sick with guilt.

When we finally got to bed, Rushie lay between us, not at the foot of the bed as usual, but pressed up against my side, shaking periodically. She stayed there the entire night. Her obvious distress made me feel even guiltier. Natalie was right; I was responsible for her injuries. What had I been thinking?

The next day we took her to our regular vet. After careful examination and a couple hundred more dollars, she said that Rushie would be just fine. We were both so relieved. That day Rushie started feeling better. She was no longer shaking. And that night she went to the foot of the bed and gave us one of her "guurrrs" when we tried to pet her. She was getting back to her old self.

Rushie: Do I ever remember that night! D and I were playing our favorite game. He threw my toy down the street-it was a good throw and I was running full speed to catch it while it was still rolling. I didn't see the car, and ran right into the tire. It knocked me down and pinched my leg between it and the pavement. It was such a shock. One second I was running and the next I was on the ground. I hit the ground so hard that I saw stars. I looked up and everything was spinning around. My leg felt like it was broken and I was bleeding.

Before I could even get up, D was there by my side. He picked me up and held me close to him. He looked at my leg and said I would be okay. I was so scared-I hardly knew what had happened. All I wanted was to be as close to D as possible.

We went into the house. M was right there making sure I was okay. D looked at my leg and wiped the blood away. I could tell by his voice that he was worried. Then M held me while D called the vet. We got into the car and drove to a hospital I'd never been to before. I hate going to the vet, for any reason, and I got even more scared when D carried me inside. D said that I was going into shock because I began shaking uncontrollably. My leg hurt so much. The vet gave me a shot that immediately made me feel better, and I relaxed a bit while he worked on my leg. When he finished he wrapped it in a bandage and M&D took me home.

We went right to bed and I tried to stay as close to D as I could. Every time I fell asleep I dreamed that I was in the street with a car speeding toward me. I'd try to get out of the way but it was too late. Just as the car was about to hit me I'd wake up and begin shaking all over again. It was a long night.

In the morning I was really sore and could hardly walk, but at least I wasn't shaking anymore. That morning M took me to my regular vet. She looked at my leg and gave me another shot. M took me home and I slept most of the day. By evening I started to feel better, although I still couldn't put any pressure on my leg, and for some reason my neck hurt.

The next day I was feeling so good I thought it was time for the bandage to come off. M made me keep it on for another week. After a while that thing drove me crazy! Then M drove me crazy by keeping me from taking it off. Finally we went back to our vet and she took the bandage off. After a few more days I was back to normal.

I wanted to start playing our game again. D didn't want to. Every night I'd get my toy and beg him to play. For the longest time, he refused. But I didn't give up–after all it is my favorite game and great exercise. Finally, one night when M wasn't home D took me out to the street and threw the toy for me. This time he threw the toy the other direction on the street and not quite as far. I know he was worried about another car coming, but he didn't need to be, because I got out of the way whenever I heard a car. I wasn't about to get hit again!

After that, D and I played our game almost every night. We were back to our old routine, and it was so much fun. Every time a car came, D would yell, "car," and I'd go to the side of the road until it passed. Then we'd start playing again. One time the same car that hit me came around the corner. It was going so fast that I hardly had time to get to get out of the way. I heard D yell. At first I thought he was yelling at me, then I realized he had yelled at the driver. When the car stopped he went up and told the driver to slow down. I think he did, because I never saw anyone drive fast around the corner again.

I know that D feels guilty about me being hit

by that car. He shouldn't. I ran right into the car. I should have been paying attention. Now I do. Plus, it is such a fun game. Playing it keeps me healthy. And it sure beats jogging!

While we are on the topic, let me tell you something about how the ring toy game is played. Correctly. First, you need a regulation ring toy. That's the one that has the bump on it. The bump makes the ring jump around when it rolls, making the game more challenging. A tennis ball won't work, nor will a ring toy without a bump. Next, you need a pitcher who can throw the toy long distances and make it roll it on its side. D is good at this. M isn't. An advanced player like me needs someone with a strong arm or there isn't enough challenge. I start running as soon as the toy is thrown. (Sometimes D pretends to throw the toy and I chase after it only to realize he didn't actually throw it. That's cheating.) I get extra points if I catch the toy before it falls over. After I catch the toy I bring it back to the pitcher, who tries to grab it from me. If the pitcher grabs it out of my mouth on the first try, I lose. If I hang on to it, I win. (I usually win.) After we play tug-of-war for a few minutes and I've proved that I can hang on to the toy, then I let go and the pitcher throws the toy again. I'm an outstanding athlete.

In addition to the ring toy game, in the summer I chase rocks and sticks when we hike and in the winter I chase snowballs when we go to the cabin. I'm not sure which is my favorite-I love all three games. As far as I'm concerned, these games are a lot like golf and skiing: they test your athletic ability, you can do it your whole life, and it's something the whole family can enjoy. I'd recommend these games to any dog and her family.

This brings me to **Rushie Rule 8**. *To be good at anything worthwhile takes dedication and practice.* When you have a game or sport that you enjoy, stick with it. I play three sports—chasing the ring toy, chasing rocks and sticks, and chasing snowballs. Each has its own rules. I am very ethical. I follow the rules carefully and don't cheat. I don't change games. I am a perfectionist and want to be good at what I do.

I'm right about most things in life and don't change my mind often. Sometimes, when you least expect it, though, you're wrong. This happened to me. Once.

Diary: *June 12, 1996.* I can't believe it. Rushie actually learned to swim!

A few weekends ago we were hiking the trail around Shaver Lake and stopped to rest and picnic near a small lagoon. The day was warm and I took my shoes off and waded in the water with Rushie. I threw a stick in to see if she would retrieve it. I threw the first one about two feet from shore. She waded out ankle deep and retrieved it without hesitation. A half-inch of water doesn't scare me, she seemed to say. I threw the sticks further and further and she ventured deeper and deeper. Before she realized it she was swimming! And they say you can't teach old dogs new tricks.

After that, Rushie was a different dog. Every time we got near water, she wanted to swim.

Last weekend, we were hiking on a trail in the Central Sierra. A creek that runs beside the trail added to the sights and sounds of a very pleasant summer morning in the mountains. Rushie would run ahead of us, find something to smell, and then lag behind as we walked by. Here we were: Natalie, Rushie and me enjoying a beautiful morning in the mountains–just like a Norman Rockwell painting on the cover of *Saturday Evening Post*. After a while we noticed something was wrong with this idyllic picture. Rushie had fallen behind. Natalie began to wonder where she was. I told her not to worry, that Rushie would catch up. Well, after several more minutes and no Rushie, we went back down the trail to find her. We walked and walked. No Rushie. Finally we came to a spur in the trail that headed toward the creek. We walked down the spur, toward the sound of water rushing over boulders, both of us worried that she might have fallen in. When we got to the creek we saw a deep, quiet pool just below the rapids. In the middle of the pool was Rushie swimming away. She looked up as we approached as if to say, "Come on in guys, the water's fine!"

After that, we began to wonder if she was a purebred fox terrier. Could she be part Lab??

Rushie: Old dogs! Part Lab? Please!

Realizing I could swim was an epiphany. It changed my life. I thank D for that.

As I mentioned, I had some very bad experiences with water when I was young and vowed never to swim again–it just seemed too dangerous.

D, with his weird sense of humor, was always trying to trick me into going into the deep water by throwing sticks or rocks and trying to get me to chase them. I love to chase sticks and rocks–but not into the water. When D threw a stick into the water I'd ignore it and think to myself, "I'm a fox terrier, not a lab. And thank God for that."

He didn't fool me with his tricks for a long, long time. But one time he did, and I'm so glad. We stayed at the cabin one summer week-end. Saturday morning, we got up early to go for a hike. We stopped near the lake about noon for lunch. I was wading in the lake and sipping the water–the sun was hot and the cool water felt good on my feet. After a while D came up and threw a stick into the lake. It was just a few inches farther out than I was, so I walked out and got it. Then he threw another stick, just a little bit farther than the last one. I went out and got that stick, too.

Then D threw another stick even farther than the last one. I walked out cautiously and grabbed it. That time the water came up to my stomach. D was having a lot of fun, and so was M. They were both saying what a good girl I was, and I started to really get into the game. D threw more sticks into the water, each one just a little farther than the last. Finally, he threw one so far into the lake that I couldn't get it and still touch the bottom. But by then I was really enjoying the game and I kept walking and grabbed the stick. I didn't realize it at the time, but I had been swimming. D threw more sticks, and I gained confidence. After getting one of the sticks, I suddenly realized that I could walk or run in the water just as if I were on land. I could keep my head up above the waves and move slowly by walking or move quickly by running.

It was liberating and exhilarating. I could swim! Suddenly, I wasn't afraid; I loved the water. The rest of that afternoon D kept throwing sticks, and I kept swimming to get them. The next day we came back to the lake, and I went straight into the water for a swim. After a while, they wanted to leave, but I still wanted to swim. They called me but I was having too much fun to get out of the water. Then they started walking on the trail as it meandered along the shore. I swam in the lake following them.

One time, not long after that, we went to the lake and D went in swimming with me. It was really fun. He'd swim out and I'd follow. We'd even race. One time, he got up on this big rock in the middle of the lake, and I got up there with him. I could see M watching from shore. We lay in the sun for a while-it was so nice and warm. Then D stood up and dove off the rock into the water. He made a big splash. It looked exciting. I went to the spot where he jumped off and stood there looking at the water. D called me. I thought to myself, "Go ahead and jump, Rushie, you're an excellent swimmer." I crouched, and then jumped as far as I could, making a big splash right in front of D. My nose went under water for a second, but I came right up and started to swim. After that, every time I saw a lake or river I wanted to jump in.

A few weekends later, we were hiking along a dusty trail on a hot summer day. There was a stream running beside the trail. I kept waiting for M&D to take a rest by the stream so I could swim. But they just kept walking and walking. They were ahead of me when I noticed a path that left the trail and went toward the stream. I thought, "What the heck, let's see where this goes." I walked down the trail and around a corner and I saw this big pool of water. It seemed to be calling me, "Rushie, come on in. The water's fine." So I did. I was having so much fun that I forgot about M&D. Then I noticed them standing on the bank. I thought they might join me, but they didn't. They just stood there smiling. Finally, I got out-I could see they wanted to go-and we started hiking again.

As I was walking up the trail, I thought about how much more fun hikes were now that I learned to swim. I had been so afraid of the water. D kept telling me not to be afraid, and kept encouraging me. For a long time, I didn't listen. Then, little by little, I overcame my fear.

This is when I discovered **Rushie Rule 9**: *Nothing is too difficult if you apply yourself.* Keep trying. Take one step at a time, and before you know it, you've accomplished something big. If I can overcome my fear of water, you can overcome your fears as well.

As I continued up the trail, I also thought it was about time for D to start throwing rocks, so I ran up ahead and turned around, hoping that he'd take the hint. Finally he did, and we began playing another one of our favorite games.

After an hour or so, we stopped at a nice campground and had a picnic lunch. We had French bread, cheddar cheese, and D's special recipe fried chicken. It was delicious! After eating and resting for a while, we walked back to the car. On the way back I took another swim.

As we were driving home I began thinking that it was about time for our annual trip to Oregon.

Diary: *August 23, 1996.* I am at SunRiver Resort near Bend, Oregon at a house we rented for the week. The whole family is here. We normally spend a week in Bend and a week in Portland. We've been doing this every year since we moved to California. It's the only time I get to see my family.

Rushie gets excited when she sees that we are packing the car and even more excited when we tell her we are going to see "Grandma and Trevor." Although the drive is exhausting for me (from Fresno it's a ten-hour drive to SunRiver and 13 hours to Portland), she never seems to get bored. She alternates between driving position and Natalie's lap and short naps in her bed in the back seat.

Rushie always seems to know where we are, even though we make this drive only once a year. When we drive directly to SunRiver, she knows when we are getting close and shows it by getting into driving position and paying careful attention to the road, undoubtedly to make sure I don't miss the turnoff. She acts the same way when we are getting close to mom's house in Portland. In neither case is it because we turn off one road onto another or because the car slows. After driving for miles on US 97, about thirty miles from the Sun-

River turnoff Rushie begins watching the road intently. As we head to Portland, despite having been on I-5 for hours, she perks up as we approach the city limits. By the time we turn off the highway and on to the surface streets that lead to mom's house, she gets on my lap and demands that I open the window so she can stick her nose out.

She knows exactly which turns to take. I tested her once by going straight when we should have turned. She was clearly distressed by my "mistake," and nuzzled my ear as if to say, "D, you missed the turn." When I turned around and made the right turn she was satisfied. When we pull into the driveway, she is the first one out of the car and heads directly to the front door. She greets mom and then walks purposefully through the house to make sure everything is as it should be. When furniture has been moved since her last visit or something is out of place, she notices and emphatically calls our attention to the anomaly.

When we get to SunRiver, she has a great time. If it is a house that we stayed in before she recognizes it. If it is a new place, she inspects with great enthusiasm.

This year, we are staying in a new house with a big deck. Rushie loves to go outside and lounge on the deck. What we didn't know was that there is a deer trail just behind the house. Every evening 10 to 15 deer pass by our deck foraging and looking for handouts. The deer are used to humans and come right up to the deck and eat grapes out of our hand.

Rushie doesn't like this one bit. The first night, she growled and barked once or twice as the deer came closer to the deck. When they kept coming, she acted as if she didn't see them, turning her head and looking the other way. Casually, without drawing attention to herself, she retreated inside the house and watched the deer on her patio from the safe side of the sliding glass door.

Rushie: I can understand why D is so impressed with my navigation skills. I've been working on them since I was a puppy, and I'm pretty good, if I do say so myself. Take me to a place once, and I know exactly where I am when I go again. I never get lost. Lots of times when we are hiking M&D forget which trail to take to get back to the car. They ask me to lead the way. I just sigh, and tell them to follow. They do, and I get us back to the car every time.

It's the same when we take trips in the car. I navigate by a combination of sight and smell. Plus, I'm blessed with a good sense of direction. I always pay attention when we go somewhere new and I memorize landmarks. It's pretty simple, really.

I love our vacations in Oregon. I get to see Grandma, Ron, Freddy, and Trevor. I like Grandma's house, and now that Lynn is gone I get to do pretty much what I want when we stay there.

Grandma's house has a nice family room and a very comfortable couch where I can take a nap or rest. Our bedroom is also nice. It is at the far end of the house, with a big, comfortable bed and a nice bathroom. At the foot of the bed is a bench that I can crawl under-like my own private cave. It's a good place to go when I want to be alone.

My favorite part of the house is the back yard. It's big enough for D and me to play with my toy, and it has a nice deck that I can sun myself on or go under and explore. I also think it's neat that the bottom half of the screen door to the back yard is torn so I can go outside any time I want. I don't know why M&D don't do that at our house. I hate having to ask every time I want to go out.

The weather in Portland is much cooler than Fresno. The sun is warm (but not hot) during the day, and the air is cool at night. The weather in SunRiver is also nice-just like Spokane's.

I like SunRiver except for the deer. They're big and unpredictable. One time I was on the deck, minding my own business, when this deer came within ten feet of me and snorted. "How rude," I thought. "This is my deck. Who asked you here anyway?" Next thing I knew, there were two more deer near the deck. D held some grapes in his hand, and one started to eat them. I even saw his tongue lick D's hand. Ugh!

I told D he shouldn't feed the deer; it encourages them. He acted as if he didn't hear me. Before you knew it there was a whole herd of deer in our back yard hoping to get some grapes. They brought their friends the next night. One even climbed up on our deck. After that I decided to go into the house and watch from the living room. I just don't understand the attraction people seem to have for deer. The ones I've seen in SunRiver are pretty obnoxious. Plus they have all sorts of diseases, fleas, and even ticks.

I like to take walks on the trails at SunRiver. There are lots of people to look at and to tell me how cute I am. One time, we had to stand on the side of the trail when a bunch of horses walked by. M kept saying, "Look, Rushie. Horsie, horsie!" As if I could have missed them. They are big and noisy, and they sweat and poop and snort. They make deer look refined. After that experience, I decided horses are more interesting when viewed from a car driving down the highway.

On one of our walks we stopped at a meadow near the Deschutes River and D let me off the leash. We'd been walking for a while and I was hot and dirty from the dust the horses kicked up. I was exploring the area when I saw a nice swimming hole. I tested the water and it was perfect. I jumped in and swam out until the current started to carry me downstream, then I swam against the current and back to shore. I did this a few times before I saw D walk up. I was hoping he'd join me for a swim, like he does sometimes. Before I could convince him to jump in M came up and made me get out of the water. I didn't mind. I had my swim and felt refreshed. M worries too much. She shouldn't. I'm an excellent swimmer. I can swim better than any lab.

Diary: *August 26, 1996.* We drove up to Mt. Bachelor today. Rushie met a Jack Russell terrier in the parking lot and played with him for a half hour–I think she met her match for energy–chasing, but never catching, the little guy.

We rode the chairlift to the mid-mountain lodge, where we had reservations for dinner. Rushie did great. She sat on the chair beside me and rode up the lift as if she'd been doing it all her life. She looked up at the mountain and down to the ground below. She seemed totally at ease. When we got to the top she hopped off the lift and started to explore, as if the ride had been the most normal thing in the world.

The only problem she had was with the grated, metal steps going up to the lodge. Because she could see through them, she couldn't understand how they could be safe to walk on. After much coaxing she finally ran up the steps to the solid deck above. After dinner we went back out on the deck where Rushie had been waiting patiently for us. Natalie offered her a snack salvaged from dinner. Rushie conducted her usual meticulous inspection of the offering before taking a bite. When she finished her snack, we crossed the deck to the top of the stairs on our way to the chairlift. Rushie took one look at the metal grates and to the ground twenty feet below and decided that she wasn't going to risk life and limb again. No amount of coaxing could change her mind. I finally picked her up and carried her down the steps. She then willingly jumped on the chairlift and looked down without fear from more than fifty feet above the ground.

Rushie: That was an exciting trip, although the food wasn't very good. I've been to Mt. Bachelor before. (D has taken me to see lots of ski areas.) Most of the time we just walk around. This time was different and much more exciting.

It started when I got out of the car and saw this cute little Jack Russell terrier. He'd just gotten back from a long hike, but still had lots of energy. After saying hello he started to run and wanted me to chase him. I'm a very fast runner, but he was amazing. Running straight I could catch him, but as soon as I started to gain he'd turn. He could turn faster than any dog I ever saw. He'd run straight and I'd start to catch up then he'd turn and I'd fall back. It was a kick.

Sometimes I wish M&D would get another dog. I like to play with D, but having my own dog to play with would be fun, too.

After that, D took me on the chairlift. It was my first time, and I was pretty excited. As we walked up to the lift I could see people getting on the chairs and riding up the mountain. It looked like an easy way to get up the hill. When we got to the chair D picked me up and held me in his arms. He sat down as the chair came up from behind. Nifty, I thought. So that's how D gets to the top of the mountain when he skis. After he got settled, he sat me down on the chair next to him. We started to move pretty fast and we were getting higher and higher off the ground. I could see the whole mountain and the ground far below. It didn't make me nervous, because I knew that D rode on these chairs all the time when he skied, and he never fell off.

When we got to the top, I hopped off and explored the area. We saw snow and D threw snowballs for me. It was a real treat getting to play in the snow in the middle of summer.

M&D walked up some steps to the deck above. I started to follow, but noticed that the steps weren't solid. I could see right through them to the ground below! I wasn't about to walk on those steps, so I just stopped. D walked back down, picked me up and put me on the first step. Surprisingly, it held my weight. Then he coaxed me up to the next step. It held, too. I quickly ran to the top, but it just didn't seem right.

After dinner M&D tried to get me to walk back down the steps. But from the top it is was long way to the ground and although the steps held once, I just didn't think it was worth the risk to trust them again. I made D carry me. His feet are bigger than mine and are less likely to slip through the cracks. I think it was the right thing to do.

By then it was getting dark, so we got on the chair lift and went down the mountain. Even though the chair is much higher off the ground than the stairs, I felt safer because the chair was solid. Isn't it odd how your mind can play tricks on you? I remember D telling M about going to the top of this tall building in Auckland, New Zealand. At the observation deck, a part of the floor was made of Plexiglas, and you could see all the way to the ground. Your mind knew it was safe to walk on the glass, but it looked dangerous. Lots of people couldn't walk on the glass. D said it took all of his willpower to make himself do it. Not wanting to walk on the grated steps doesn't seem so strange to me.

One of the nicest things about our vacations in Oregon is that we are with D's family. I am family oriented. I like it when the family is together-the more the better. I especially like being around Freddy and was excited when he came to live with us while he was going to college. As it turned out, it was harder to get along with Freddy when he was living with us than when he was visiting.

Diary. *November 20, 1996*. There's conflict in our household involving my wife, my son, and my dog. As hard as I've tried, I haven't been able to resolve it. It all began when Freddy decided to live with us and attend Fresno State.

Having Freddy move in with us now seems ironic. When we lived in L. A. Freddy stayed with us all summer and sometimes brought his friends. Our L. A. house was small, so when we moved to Spokane, we bought a big house with plenty of space for Freddy and his friends. Ironically, he didn't visit often and we didn't need the extra space. When we moved to Fresno we bought a smaller house, because there were just the two of us and Rushie.

Well, we barely got settled into our new house when Freddy decided that he wanted to attend Fresno State and–you guessed it–move in with us. A dog and three people in a three-bedroom house–especially when one of the people is an 18 year old–can feel pretty cramped.

Freddy has a lot of energy and a loud voice. When he talks on the phone, he paces. And he talks on the phone incessantly. Freddy can't go half an hour without talking to someone. If a friend doesn't call him, he calls a friend. No matter where Natalie is in the house, sooner or later Freddy will walk by talking loudly. After getting the "look" from Natalie, he reluctantly hangs up the phone and goes back to his studies.

Natalie, who teaches part time at Fresno State, works best alone with jazz quietly playing in the background. With Freddy there, she can't get away from the conversation and has a hard time concentrating.

Rushie was in heaven when Freddy moved in with us and followed him wherever he went. The noise doesn't bother her at all. But, when Freddy began interfering with her security duties, she had a problem.

As part of her routine after breakfast, she retreats to her spot on top of the couch in front of a window that looks out onto the street. From that vantage point, she can monitor the traffic and guard the house against intruders.

Freddy's bedroom quickly became so strewn with clothes, golf clubs, and other debris that he began to use the den to do his schoolwork. Rushie guards the house from the den, but is content to share the room with Freddy. The problem is that Freddy doesn't always reciprocate.

Some of Rushie's habits get on Freddy's nerves. Rushie is a nail biter–a habit she may have picked up from Natalie. The difference is that Natalie is a stealth biter (the only way I know that she bites her nails is because they never grow), while Rushie is a chomper. When she decides that she needs a manicure, she goes to work by methodically biting each of her nails, one at a time. The crunching and gnashing are audible to anyone within a thirty-foot radius.

The cycle of complaints starts with Natalie complaining to me about Freddy. I talk to Freddy and he complains about my "neurotic" dog keeping him from his studies. I talk to Rushie, but she is committed to her job and refuses to change. What to do?

Rushie. I love Freddy. He is so much fun to be around. He's always joking and playing with me. I was excited when he moved into our house. At first I tried to sleep with him on his bed at night. Going into his room, with all the stuff lying around on the floor reminded me of camping out. I'd get to jump over shirts and shoes and socks before getting to the bed. If he were already in bed, I'd say hello by politely nuzzling his ear with my nose. I could tell he didn't like that very much because he'd try to pull the covers up over his head before I could reach him. It turned out to be a fun game. I'd see that he went to bed, and if the door was open I'd sneak down the hall, race through the door, jump across the clothes and up onto the bed, and try to nuzzle him before he could pull the covers up. Sometimes he'd yell; other times he'd just groan. After that, I'd usually lie down at the foot of his bed and go to sleep.

In the middle of the night I'd get up and go into M&D's room and sleep at the foot of their bed. Then in the morning, if Freddy's door was open, I'd run in and jump on the bed to wake him. He usually put his head under the covers when I did that, and I had fun walking on top of him.

I didn't realize it until he moved in, but Freddy can be pretty crabby in the morning, and sometimes he'd yell and chase me out of the room. One morning, after he chased me out, M let me back in. He yelled at me and sounded really mad. I felt better when I heard M laugh.

My primary responsibility as chief of security is to guard the house. The best place to watch for intruders is on the couch in front of the window in the den. From that vantage point I have a full view of the entire front yard and street and can see any approaching intruder. Every morning after breakfast I go to my post and spend the entire morning on the job. I do this in good weather and bad, when I feel good and when I'm sick, when I'm refreshed and when I'm tired. It's my job.

When Freddy moved in, he began spending a lot of time in the den studying. I didn't mind. He'd do his job and I'd do mine. The next thing I knew, he'd tell me to be quiet. Quiet about what, I thought? I wasn't barking or making noise. I was just sitting there doing my job.

Sure, I sometimes give myself a manicure while I'm working, but I don't see how that could bother anyone. One day, while I was guarding the house and giving myself a manicure, Freddy began yelling at me, calling me all sorts of names, saying I was "neurotic." I didn't pay much attention to his rants and continued about my business. (Sometimes when people are acting irrationally it's best to just ignore them.) The next thing I knew he picked me up, put me down in the hall, and shut the door so I couldn't get back to my post.

That seemed pretty rude to me, but instead of confronting him about it, I went into the other room and waited for him to come out. When he did, I went into the den and back to my post. The rest of the day was okay. He studied. I guarded.

The next day he yelled at me and again threw me out of the den. It was peak guarding time, just before the mail carrier was due. That made me mad. He was interfering with my job. So I pushed the door open and got back in position. He threw me out again! I couldn't believe it. But I can be pretty determined, so I waited at the end of the hall, and when he left the room to get some coffee I went back in and got into position. No one, I thought, was going to keep me from doing my job. Not even Freddy.

From then on, as soon as I finished breakfast, I went directly to the den and started to guard the house. If Freddy threw me out, I'd wait until he left and go right back in. After a while I think he got the message because he quit throwing me out of the room. I did notice, however, that when I started to give myself a manicure sometimes he would leave, which was fine with me.

At the time I got pretty mad at Freddy for interfering with my job and for treating household security so lightly. Looking back I realize that he was young and inexperienced-you know how teenagers are, they think they already know everything and don't listen to anyone. But Freddy is an intelligent person, and I'm happy to say he ultimately followed in my footsteps. After he graduated from college, he took a job with one of the finest security companies in the nation and now is an expert in commercial security systems.

I am a very sophisticated dog. I've spent a lot of time around humans and understand what they expect. There's nothing more frustrating to me than to do what I know is right and to be criticized for my efforts.

Diary: *August 15, 1997.* Rushie can be such a brat! We just got back from vacation in Oregon. While we were there we went to the coast with mom, Ron, and Trevor, and we stayed in a small cabin right on the ocean. The weather was nice for the Oregon coast (meaning that it wasn't raining), and we were looking forward to an enjoyable time playing golf, walking on the beach, and generally enjoying each other's company.

We met in Portland at my mom's house, but took two cars–Mom, Ron and Trevor in one car and Natalie, Rushie and me in the other. The dogs hadn't been together much in Portland, but when they were Rushie was her usual bossy self and had Trevor totally intimidated.

When we got to the close confines of the beach cabin, Rushie turned into an ogre. She growled at Trevor, stood on him, and finally banished him to a corner under a table. Every time he tried to come out, she would growl, and he would retreat. Ron was humiliated that his dog was allowing himself to be bullied, and I was embarrassed by her behavior.

I tried to discipline her, but it didn't do much good. Rushie's goal seemed to be to keep Trevor in the corner under the table whenever he was in the cabin. The only time she let him alone was when they were outside. And that was mainly because they liked to do different things. Rushie stayed close and walked with us, while Trevor, the hunter, ran all over the beach picking up whatever stray scents were available.

We walked along the shore until we reached a cove with rocks and tide pools. Rushie decided it was time for a swim. She had a grand time swimming and bobbing in the small waves that were created as the water washed over the rocks. I found a stick and threw it out into the surf. She ran after it and swam through the waves and out into the ocean. She got the stick and brought it part way back, dropped it in the water, then expected me to find and throw another stick.

Rushie: I don't like this name-calling. I am not a brat. In fact, I'm one of the best-behaved dogs ever. That was a very small

cabin, too small to have a bunch of dogs running around. Trevor is pretty big and very un-
gainly. I knew that if I let him have his way
he'd knock over chairs and spill glasses. Did
anyone want that to happen?

When we got to the beach and I saw how small
our cabin was, I knew I'd have to be strict
with Trevor. Sure, I growled a lot, but I
blame Trevor for that. He should just do what
I say. He knows that I am in charge. But every
time I see him I need to show him again who's
boss. Frankly, although he's a nice guy, he's
not the sharpest tool in the shed. He's certainly not at my level.

You'll have to admit, D, that I did get Trevor
to behave. If it hadn't been for me, he'd have
run wildly around the cabin breaking things
and making a mess.

Everyone had fun on the beach. Trevor is a
good runner and loves to follow scents on the
beach. I like to run, but don't go as far. I'd
rather walk with M&D and try to get D to chase
me or throw rocks and sticks for me to chase.

I was completely relaxed and enjoying my walk
when a large dog came up. Well, as you know, I
don't like large dogs much and I especially
don't like them sniffing me. I stayed calm and
greeted him politely but in a way that made it
clear I wasn't interested in getting to know
him. He left after a minute or two. I thought
that I handled the situation pretty well, much
better than when I panicked the first time D
and I went to the beach.

We walked on the sand for a while until we got to a place where there were pools of water. I jumped in. Wow, was that water cold! At one end the water crashed over some rocks and made waves that were fun to swim in. I bobbed on top of the water just like the sticks that D threw. Then I got him to throw sticks into the ocean for me to chase. I just love to jump the waves. D wonders why I don't bring the sticks back to him. The reason is that this is my game and I make the rules. I like to grab the stick, just to prove that I can, but once I've done that what's the point of bringing it back to him? Even a lab could do that.

I've tried to teach Trevor to swim, but he's afraid. Trevor's getting up there in years and, as the saying goes, it's hard to teach old dogs new tricks.

I later learned that if it is hard for some dogs to learn something new, it is equally hard for some humans. This next diary entry illustrates my point.

Diary: *December 3, 1997.* Recently, when Natalie was visiting her brother, David, he said that dogs distinguish between people and dogs by their behavior rather than their appearance. To demonstrate, he got down on all fours and "barked" at Rushie. Rushie looked at him quizzically at first, then barked in return. Dave thought that he had proved his point, and Natalie was dismayed that her smart puppy might not be as smart as she thought. When she later told me about the incident, I said that just because Rushie barked at Dave doesn't mean that she thought he was a dog. But it did get me to thinking that we might be reading too much humanness into Rushie's behavior. We know that dogs think and feel–but at what level of complexity? I think that many empty nesters like Natalie and me anthropomorphize our pet's behavior.

Rushie: Anthropomorphize? Spare me, please. Leave it to the philosophers to raise questions about how we can know what other beings think. You're out of your depth.

I barked at Dave because he was acting so silly. Who ever heard of a person getting down on all fours and barking like a dog? It's ridiculous. And he doesn't even do a good dog imitation. All I was trying to say was, "Don't be so goofy, Dave. If you want to play, get my toy."

But you do raise an important question about how dogs feel. I realize that I am smarter than most dogs and even some humans. (D says the professors he works with are very smart, and he's had some of them to our house for dinner. I can tell you from direct experience that professors can be pretty dumb. At one party an economics professor started talking to a room full of people. One by one they slipped away until there was only one person left, and this guy never took a breath! At least I am smart enough to know when people are not interested in me.)

Still, in many ways dogs and humans are alike. Forget me for a minute and think about the average dog. They like to play games just like humans do. (Playing fetch is a favorite game of dogs. I don't fetch.) They get happy and sad and often are happy or sad with their owners. Dogs have a sense of humor, just like humans. (Why do you think so many dogs like to play keep-away?) Dogs have jobs, just like humans-mine is household security. They need affection and appreciate praise. They love and are loyal to the people who love them. Dogs who are raised with over-indulgent parents get spoiled just like children. They feel guilty when they do something wrong and happy when they do something right. Although dogs can't speak, they understand humans. They learn many words and can understand human wants and emotions. Humans and dogs get along well because they share so many emotions and feelings.

I am fortunate that M&D provided a nurturing environment. When I was a puppy, they talked to me and taught me right from wrong. They respected me and let me develop my own personality. They played with me and encouraged me to have fun. They supported my decision to work in household security. I owe them a great deal.

M&D may be good but they aren't perfect. In fact, they can be pretty dense. For example, it took me years to teach them that I do not need to be bathed in the bathtub.

Diary: *March 12, 1998.* Rushie has this strange love/hate relationship with water. She loves to play in the water, but give her a bath in the tub and she is in misery. Every time I bathe her she cowers and shakes uncontrollably until I'm done. The only part of the bathing process she enjoys is attacking the towel when we dry her off.

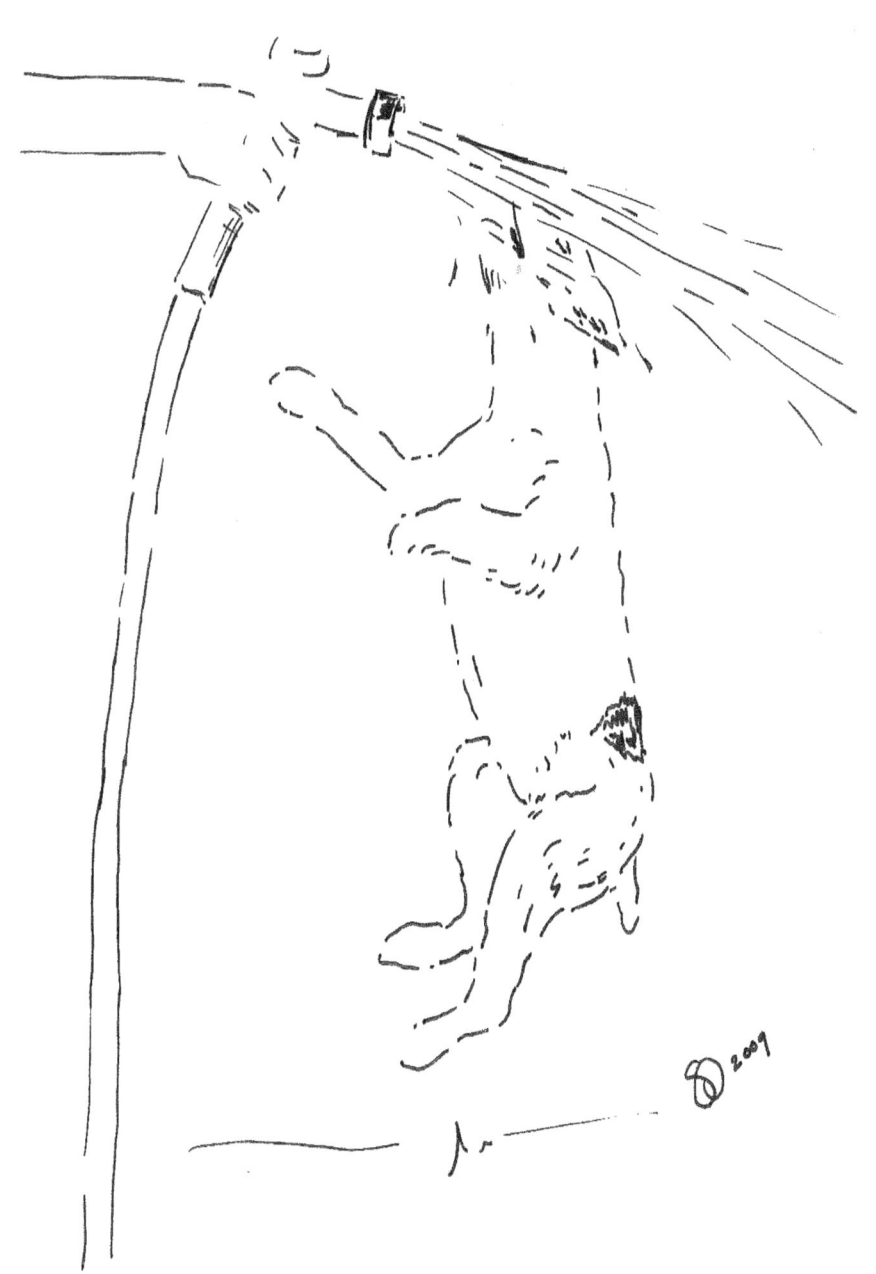

The bath is such a miserable experience for her that we bathe her only when she absolutely needs it, which given the ordeal, isn't often.

One day I was in the driveway washing my car. Rushie was in the house whining to get out so she could play in the water. After I finished my car, I let her out so she could play in the water while I squirted her. After a few minutes she was soaking wet. As she looked up at me with her big, brown eyes sparkling and water dripping down her nose I had an inspiration: why not give her a bath at the same time? I got the soap and lathered her up. She didn't mind the soap, as long as I didn't take too long. After I'd finished I went back to squirting her with the hose, at the same time rinsing her off. Voila! She finally got a bath she enjoyed.

After I soaped her down and rinsed her off I said, "Good Rushie. Good bath!" The next weekend, I asked if she wanted a bath–a word that normally would cause her to hide under the bed. Instead, she looked at me quizzically for a moment, and then walked toward the garage, indicating that she wanted to go to the driveway where we played in the water. I took her outside and squirted her with the hose, giving her a bath at the same time. After that she'd get so excited when we asked her if she wanted a bath that we started to spell the word, so we'd have time to get the soap and hose ready. Soon Rushie learned to spell bath so we abbreviated it to "b a." She learned that after a few times as well. Finally, we resorted to whispering our intentions. The lengths one has to go when your dog can spell!

Rushie: I hate tub baths! I get soap in my eyes and water up my nose. The only good part is drying off, when I bite and play tug of war with the towel. I don't worry about getting a tub bath any more now because D always washes me with the hose.

Playing in the water while D squirts me with the hose is one of my favorite games–I've been addicted to it since I was a puppy. It's especially fun on hot summer evenings in Fresno.

I don't mind D lathering me with soap while we are playing; it's not really part of the game but it sure beats bathing in the tub. I usually play in the hose and get a bath after D washes his car, once a week or so. There are only two things wrong with these baths. First, they don't happen often enough. (D should wash his car more often–I hate to be seen in a dirty car.) Second, they don't last long enough. (Before you know it, I've swallowed so much water that my stomach hurts and I have to quit.)

D and I don't go places without M very often, but M and I go places without D all the time. When we go on a trip or a hike, for instance, it's almost always the three of us. One weekend D and I went to the cabin and M stayed home. It turned out to be a weekend I'll never forget.

Diary: *October 13, 1999.* Natalie had to work so Rushie and I went to the cabin by ourselves last weekend. Rushie was delighted to go with me, but Natalie, as usual, hated to be away from Rushie. Not only does she get lonely, she worries that am not careful enough and something will happen to her "baby." She knows I love Rushie as much as she does, but thinks I'll let her off the leash (which I do) and she'll get hit by a car or lost on a hike. Or, most dangerous of all when we are at the cabin, get attacked by a coyote.

Rushie, on the other hand, loves to go places with just me. She knows that she'll get to do things that she ordinarily wouldn't. It reminds me of when as a young boy I went on fishing trips with my dad. I'd know that it was going to be different and fun, and the apprehension I detected in my mother made me believe that dad and I were co-conspirators in some slightly dangerous but very intriguing plot. I think Rushie felt the same way last weekend when she realized that we were going to the cabin alone–without Natalie.

When I got home from work Friday I decided to go to the cabin, even though Natalie couldn't. I also decided to take the dog, which delighted Rushie and worried Natalie. As I was backing the car out of the driveway with Rushie beside me in driving position Natalie said sternly, "Be careful. Remember that at this time of year there are lots of coyotes. Don't let Rushie outside without watching her."

"We'll be careful," I said, thinking there was no danger. Was I ever wrong!

Rushie: Do I remember that trip! It was a Friday night in the fall, and I was preparing for another boring weekend at home. I was sitting on the sofa in the den, looking out onto the street, thinking about not doing anything all weekend and getting sleepy at the thought. I had just started to drift off when I heard the garage door open. That meant D was home. So I got up and slowly started to walk into the den to say hi.

(I try to greet M&D when they come home after they've been gone for a while. They seem to like it and are excited to see me. And, after being alone for a long time, it's nice to have company. I like it best when both M and D come home at the same time. Still, I have my limits. When they've been gone for only a short time and I'm sleepy I usually don't get up. The funny thing is that they look for me.

Sometimes, after she's been gone only a few minutes, M will make a big deal about seeing me, and say in a loud voice, "Hi, Rushie. How've you been doing? I'm so glad to see you!" When she does that I sometimes play along and pretend to be glad to see her. I don't want to hurt her feelings. It does seem silly, however.)

D walked in from the garage and I could see that he was in a good mood. He reached down and rubbed my ears and said, "I think we should go to the cabin-in-the-woods!" That got my attention, but because M hadn't packed any-thing I figured that he might be kidding. When D changed into his jeans and put on his boots, I started to get excited, thinking that maybe we would go after all.

Then I noticed that M hadn't changed her clothes and still hadn't packed anything. I wondered what was happening. D began putting some stuff in the car, and I knew he was go-ing. I first got excited that I might get to go, then worried that I'd have to stay home with M. I thought it best to stay close to D to make sure he knew I wanted to go; I fol-lowed him in and out of the house as he packed the car.

He didn't pack much and was ready to go in no time. And I'm always ready to go to the cabin. Then, M picked me up and held me in her arms. I figured that was that–I was in for another long weekend at home. When D walked up and took me from M and put me in the car I was really excited and happy.

M had a severe look on her face and I thought she might reach in and grab me, so I got into driving position and told D to get going before she could change her mind. He must have paid attention because he got in, started the engine, and said goodbye to M through the window. M said something to me, too, but I didn't listen. I just wanted to get out of there! D backed out of the driveway and we were on our way.

I was really happy because I knew the weekend was going to be a lot more fun than I expected. I like being with D almost as much as being with M and D together because he treats me like an adult. He lets me do what I want most of the time and doesn't try to get me to do everything his way. I don't always have to be on a leash. And he likes to play with me. Also, when I'm with D I feel safe. He's strong and not afraid of anything.

As we drove off I was thinking that D and I would have an adventure-filled weekend. Little did I know how much adventure there would be.

When I'm in driving position I watch the road carefully. Lots of times I'll see another dog or a cat. I usually growl, just to let them know that they would be in big trouble if I weren't trapped in the car. This time I saw only one dog as we left. I gave him a deep growl, and I could tell that he was scared. (I can be pretty intimidating.)

I got on D's lap when we turned onto the four-lane road that begins the steep climb up the mountain. Although it was only mid-October, I looked for snow on the side of the road. When I saw the first signs of snow I put my nose close to the window. (D doesn't like me to put my nose on the window because it makes spots, so when we are driving and I want him to open the window I put my nose really close and he usually opens it.) With the window open, my nostrils filled with the wonderful smells of the mountains.

At the end of the four-lane the road narrows and begins to wind its way up to Shaver Lake. The smell of the trees gets stronger. Most of the time I also smell wild animals, and sometimes I see a deer or a coyote crossing the road. The closer we get to the cabin the more excited I get. As soon as D stops the car I prepare to get out. It is very important to get out first-it's part of my security protocol. I don't want D to walk around and get his smell all over everything before I've had a chance to find out who and what has been there. That night, even before I got out of the car, I could smell coyote.

D got his bag out of the car, walked to the front door and opened it. I went in first and looked around the cabin to be sure that everything was in its proper place and that there were no intruders, then went back outside and helped D finish unloading. I noticed that the smell of coyote was still pretty strong. Once back inside, I went out on the deck to check the back of the house. The scent of coyote was strong even there. "How dare they trespass on my property!" I thought. I growled and barked to scare them off. After I was sure they'd gone, I came inside and got up on the couch as D lit a fire in the fireplace.

Then, I thought I should check the front yard again, just as a precaution. I didn't want to wake up in the middle of the night with the cabin surrounded by coyotes. I had D let me outside. I made sure that he left the door ajar because I was expecting trouble.

I proceeded cautiously. I stood at the top of the stairs for a couple of minutes looking around and sniffing the air. I couldn't see much because it was dark, but the smell of coyote wasn't any stronger than before, I barked a few times then relaxed a bit, certain I'd scared them away. I walked down the stairs and out into the blackness of the yard. I went to the bathroom and sniffed some more.

Just as I started to relax, I heard a noise-a slight rustling of the grass-I looked up and there was the biggest, scariest wolf standing not 20 feet away, ready to pounce. (D says it was a coyote, but I know better. Coyotes don't get that big.) His teeth were showing and he was drooling. Two thoughts flashed through my mind. Should I attack and try to defeat this monster or should I run back to the house and warn D. If I fought and lost, I would put D in danger. I decided to warn D.

I turned and ran with the giant wolf right be-hind me. I could hear him breathing and thought he was going to catch me before I could reach the door. My only thought was to make it to the house so I could warn D. As I ran up the stairs I could hear his jaws snap. Miraculously he missed. Then, the porch light went on. (Every time I go up the stairs it goes on. I haven't quite figured out why, but it is handy.) The light seemed to startle him and slowed him down just enough that he missed on his last vicious attempt to grab me. I hit the door at full speed–thank goodness it was still open–and ran into the house. I got behind D ready to fight if that evil wolf came into the house.

D was already up and heading toward the door when I came in. He asked if I was okay. I was. He got a flashlight and went back outside onto the porch. That worried me. What if the wolf was still out there? How would we get home if the wolf attacked and D couldn't drive? I followed him onto the porch at full Level 4 Alert. I'm sure my barking and growling kept the wolf from attacking again.

D pointed the flashlight beam on the yard, then on the hill across the street. At first I couldn't see anything. Then I saw the wolf's evil eyes glowing in the flashlight beam. As soon as I saw them they were gone, but I knew he was out there, and I knew that I needed to remain vigilant.

D and I stood outside a few minutes longer. I gave that wolf one last vicious growl and bark before I went back into the house. D picked me up and gave my head and ears a rub. By then I felt pretty good because I had really scared that wolf.

After that, whenever I went outside the cabin at night at, D or M went with me. I think that they wanted to make sure they were close to me in case a coyote or wolf came back. They know that when I bark and growl wolves and coyotes run. I think it makes them feel safe.

Smart. Attractive. Graceful. A wire fox terrier is the perfect dog. But potential owners beware: we have a mind of our own.

Diary: *June 23, 2000.* Big dogs are fine outside, but in the house at night, when you are reading the paper after work, they lay at your feet not at your side or in your lap. If you like to have your dog close, at 20 pounds and 16 inches, fox terriers are the perfect size. Rushie has the endurance to go on long hikes, and the strength to roughhouse with my son, but still is small enough to sit on my lap or hold in my arms.

The problem is that Rushie isn't very affectionate. As a puppy, she liked to be close to Natalie, but the older she got, the less tolerant she became of the hugs and kisses and squeezes that are her specialty. One of Natalie's favorite things is to hold Rushie close when she goes to bed at night. As a pup, Rushie would curl up with her back to Natalie's stomach and sleep all night under the covers. The older she got the less interested she became in cuddling at night. Natalie, however, could never give up trying for a little affection.

The ritual is the same night after night. I go to bed to read. Natalie gives Rushie a treat. Rushie brings the treat to bed and I read while Rushie chews. Natalie normally comes to bed later and grabs Rushie and hauls her to the top of the bed to hold her close. If Rushie doesn't jump off the bed to escape Natalie's grasp, she lies there and endures, like a prisoner of war being tortured. As she approaches her limit of tolerance she starts to huff and puff and breath rapidly through her nose. Then she struggles in earnest to free herself of this indignity and returns to the foot of the bed–as far away from us as possible.

I finally tried to convince Natalie not to try to hold Rushie in bed at night because it was clear that she hated it. Natalie can control herself for a week or two then gives in to the urge, and the ritual is played out again.

Rushie: I try to be a good member of the family. I work hard, do what I'm told (most of the time), and try to be a good companion. I love to ride in the car and am an excellent navigator. I go on walks with M (when it's not too hot). I help greet the guests when they come to our house. When M&D want me to show off, I go through my trick routine flawlessly. But I'm not a touchy-feely type of dog. A kind word, cheerful greeting, and pat on the head or a scratch on the stomach are sufficient. I'm grown up and independent and don't need the constant touching and petting that I craved as a puppy.

I like being home at night. I quit work about 7:00 p.m. (I've found that the most productive guarding is between 8:00 a.m. and 2:00 p.m. After that, I turn the responsibility over to M and take a short nap. I'm available again from about 5:00 p.m. to 7:00 p.m.) D gives me dinner about eight and I snack with them when they eat at about nine. After snacks I get up on the sofa and lie down between them. This is my idea of togetherness. I am content with D on one side of me and M on the other. We talk a bit, and I even let them give me an occasional pat on the back. But please, don't grab me. Don't maul me. Don't squeeze me. I am not a baby. Give me my space!

I look forward to going to bed with D. He reads, I get a pig's ear to chew, and we spend quality time together. I chew the pig's ear at the foot of the bed. He doesn't try to grab me or maul me. He reads. I chew. Period. We have an understanding.

About an hour later M comes to bed. I've finished my chew, and I'm starting to get sleepy. I get nervous when M pulls back the covers to get into bed because I know she'll try to grab me. Sometimes, I just lie there and hope for the best. Other times, I jump off the bed and lie on the floor in the corner. Lately, I've tried mental telepathy. I repeat over and over in my mind, "Don't grab me. Don't touch me. Leave me alone to sleep and dream in peace!"

Sometimes it works; sometimes it doesn't.

Sometimes she catches me and pulls me up to the top of the bed where she smothers me with hugs and kisses. Occasionally even D gets in on the act. They turn me on my back and D rubs my stomach. It feels good, and I relent for a minute or two. Then I think about being trapped. I think about being under the covers and hot, not being able to sleep. The room feels like it is closing in on me. My heart starts beating faster. My breathing becomes labored. I start to panic. "Enough," I think, "I have to escape." With all of my strength I twist and turn and struggle to break free.

Then I go to the bottom of the bed-as far away from M's grasp as possible.

I know I sometimes hurt M's feelings by not sleeping next to her, but I can't help myself. I panic. It's not that I don't love you, M, it's just that I need my space. And my dignity.

It's not only my dignity that concerns me. I'm also concerned about my health. Ever since I moved to Fresno, I've had allergies. They seem to be getting worse. I itch all the time now and it's worse when I get hot. I could tell M&D were also worried. M eventually took me to an allergist. What a humiliating experience that turned out to be!

Diary: *September30, 2000*. Poor Rushie and her skin problems. After many failed treatments, the vet thought it might be an allergy. Natalie took her to a specialist who gave her an allergy test.

I knew Natalie was going to take Rushie to the allergist that morning but wasn't prepared for what I saw when I got home from work that evening. I opened the door expecting Rushie to greet me. She didn't. I looked around, called her name, and finally saw her lying on the couch with a forlorn expression on her face. I walked over to give her a pat on the head. She looked up and seemed to smile. Then I saw the hairless patch where the vet had shaved her fur to do the tests. I had to laugh. She looked like a failed medical experiment. Apparently Rushie didn't see the humor in her situation. The forlorn look returned; she got down from the couch and walked into the other room without another glance at me.

Rushie: I've been feeling terrible the last few months. Every time I turn around M is taking me to the vet, which I absolutely hate.

They put me on an examination table like a piece of meat. The vet, some guy I don't even know, pokes me, and looks in my mouth and other openings too embarrassing to mention. He sticks me with a needle, gives M some pills, and sends me home. Morning and night M holds my mouth open and forces pills down my throat. She sticks her fingers in so far it makes me gag.

I still don't feel good and I still itch!

Then, M took me to a vet in Oakdale, about a two-hour drive from our house. That was one of the most humiliating experiences of my life. When we pulled up to the office and I got out of the car I immediately smelled the distinctive odor of sick animals-one of the things I hate most about the vet's. Naturally I didn't want to go in, but M just picked me up and carried me. She put me on a table, and this guy came up and started to shave the fur on my right side. I could tell by his smell that he was a vet. (Vets always smell like sick animals.) Then, he stuck a bunch of needles into my side. After a few minutes the spots where he stuck the needles started to itch, but M wouldn't let me scratch them. Later, the doctor came back and looked at my side. Finally, M picked me up and took me back to the car for the two-hour ride home. By that time, I was feeling so miserable I couldn't even enjoy the ride.

On the way home, M told me that the vet said I wasn't allergic to anything except pollen. Pollen! Great, I thought, we live in the agricultural capital of the U.S., and the "only" thing I'm allergic to is pollen. They might as well say that I'm allergic to Fresno.

When I got home I went straight to the sofa to rest. Then D came home and started to laugh at me! What a weird and perverted sense of humor he has. I didn't really feel like being treated so rudely so I left and went to the den where I could rest in peace. I fell asleep and dreamed about racing through the fields and swimming in the lake. I didn't itch when I was dreaming and felt better when I woke up.

I love to go on trips, and I love to go skiing in Utah. The cool air feels good on my skin, and we usually get to play in the snow. I like being around M's relatives, but Daisy, the dog that M's niece Morgana has, is not a good hostess.

Diary: *January 13, 2001.* We spent Christmas in Utah skiing and visiting relatives. We stayed with Natalie's niece Morgana and her dog Daisy. The contrast between Rushie and Daisy is striking and made me realize how unusual Rushie is.

For one thing, Rushie is really smart. I'll bet she knows at least 500 words. She doesn't always react when she hears a word because she knows that it isn't being used in a meaningful context. If we are driving in the car and I say, "Rushie, do you want a bath?" She will just look at me without reacting as if to say, "You're kidding. Surely you know there's no hose in the car!" But if I say the same thing at home, she'll go crazy.

I think that her intelligence is a big part of why she is so unusual. She has trouble relating to other dogs as equals, because she believes, as my mother once said, that she is an "evolutionary step above normal dogs." I think much of the trouble Rushie has with other dogs derives from the fact that she feels superior to them and doesn't hide her feelings.

Rushie: An "evolutionary step above normal dogs." I like that. Grandma is very perceptive. Actually I do not consider mere dogs my equal. I find that most dogs are not very smart or interesting. I'd much rather be around humans.

Look at the matter from my perspective. I don't mean to brag, but I am very attractive, especially after I've had a clip. Whenever I meet a new human the first thing they say is, "What a cute dog!" It may be superficial, but comments like that make me feel special.

What happens when I meet a dog? They don't say anything and hardly look at me because they are in such a hurry to sniff my rear! Yuk! How would you like some mangy dog off the street sniffing you? I've seen how humans react when dogs sniff them-they get all embarrassed and push him away as fast as possible. Get my point?

I have a distant cousin I see on occasion. She is a Dalmatian named Daisy. Daisy is about the most uncouth and ignorant dog I've ever met. She makes Trevor seem like a Harvard graduate. It's not her fault, really. She lives outside and doesn't have much human contact. She has no idea of how to behave inside a house.

When we first met I tried to be friends, but she plays too roughly and never listens. I try to discipline her, but she either ignores me or gets mad.

Let me give you an example from the time we spent Christmas in Utah. We stayed at Morgana's house in a room in the basement. All of our stuff was in that room-suitcases, shoes, clothes, D's skis, everything. That was where we slept and where I hung out when I wanted to be alone. It was my sanctuary.

Daisy showed no consideration whatsoever. Every time I left the room, she went in and rummaged through our things. I couldn't stand guard the whole time, and every time I left Daisy snuck into my room. I was at my wits' end with this dog. I told her to keep out in the strongest terms I could. I growled, I barked, I threatened. This dog, with no formal education or proper upbringing, knew no etiquette and refused to pay attention. Finally- I'm not proud of this-I peed on the floor in front of the door, thinking this was the only language she would understand.

This still didn't keep her out of the room! And to make matters worse, M&D got mad at me. They didn't even seem to care that Daisy came in our room. I was so frustrated. The next day I peed on the floor again. All it got me was another lecture from M. It didn't deter Daisy one bit.

I know, I know. This was Daisy's house, not mine. But I didn't ask to stay there-we were invited guests. Besides, Daisy is an outside dog and was in the house only because I was.

After two long of days of increasing tension, they finally put Daisy outside where she belonged. After that I would go to the sliding glass door to the back yard and stand there until Daisy noticed me. Then, I would walk back and forth in front of the door and tell her, "Now you see why you should listen to me. I don't live here, but I am in the house and you're not. If you treated me like a proper guest, you would still be in the house. I hope you have learned your lesson."

She hadn't. Every time she was let back in the house she became insufferable and possessive. Soon she'd have to go outside again. I'd go to the sliding glass door and look at her with combination of disgust and pity, realizing how important education and a certain level of sophistication are in getting along in this world.

Unfortunately most dogs are not very refined-they don't know what they don't know-and they refuse to listen to someone who does.

On the other hand, being around humans sometimes requires acting silly. I can act as silly as any human.

Diary: *January 13, 2001 (continued)*. On Christmas Eve Natalie dressed Rushie in a Santa suit. She looked so cute in her red hat and beard, with "arms" out to the side and pant legs around her front feet. From the front she looked like a small Santa. She willingly stayed in costume the entire evening.

Rushie: I don't mind dressing up. M put the Santa suit on me, and I could tell that everyone liked it so I decided to keep it on. I walked around so that everyone could see me, and then I got up on the couch, sat down, with my "arm" on the armrest. From the front I looked like a little Santa sitting there relaxing on Christmas Eve.

I know I looked a bit silly, but what the heck, it was Christmas and I was celebrating like everyone else.

This wasn't the first time M dressed me up. Another time she bought a witch costume, with a big, pointy hat, a skirt, and a broom. From the front I looked like a real witch. On Halloween night, when the neighborhood kids knocked on our door to trick-or-treat, I hid behind the corner out of sight, and when M opened the door I ran up and scared them with a bark. It was a lot of fun.

Sometimes M will let me wear one of her necklaces. I enjoy that especially after I've had a clip and a bath. Just because I'm in the security business doesn't mean that I'm not in touch with my feminine side or that I don't like to feel pretty.

Lots of dogs would be offended if anyone tried to dress them up like M does. But I like to play human games. Not all dogs have the intelligence and sophistication to do this.

After dinner at Morgana's house on Christmas Eve I walked by the sliding glass doors to the back yard several times just to make sure Daisy saw me in costume. I wanted her to know what she was missing, although I doubt she understood what it all meant.

Very intelligent dogs, like very intelligent people, sometimes have difficulty adapting to certain social situations. Humans expect dogs to be followers.

Some dogs are leaders. I am a leader. M&D have difficulty grasping that fact.

Diary: *June 3, 2001.* I've been reading about dogs lately in an attempt to understand Rushie better. As descendents from the wolf, they have many of the same instincts as wolves do. Primary among them is the pack instinct. The idea is that dogs identify with humans as members of the same pack. A pack has a hierarchy, a leader and followers. Normally, dogs are followers and the human members of the pack are leaders.

I'm not sure that Rushie understands this. Most of the time she acts as if she thinks she is the pack leader. She leads on walks, she decides when she gives affection, and generally plans her own day around tasks she has defined. She acts as if she thinks that Natalie and I are there primarily to attend to her needs.

Dog experts believe that this isn't natural, and a dog that doesn't accept human leadership is likely to be neurotic and maladjusted. Although saying Rushie is neurotic and maladjusted seems extreme, I wouldn't call her normal, either. She certainly believes she's queen of the household.

Rushie: M&D are constantly trying to psychoanalyze me. I "do" this because I "think" that. Most of the time they don't have a clue about what I am really thinking. And when they start to consult "experts" on dog behavior they usually get even farther off track. It's time for a dog's perspective.

Experts try to explain dog behavior by the behavior of our wolf ancestors. Sure, dogs share their ancestry with wolves, but dogs are different from wolves just like humans are different from monkeys. Wolves grow up in the wild and never see humans. Dogs and humans have evolved together over thousands of years, and because of this dogs can think like humans. Wolves are wild animals. Dogs are civilized.

Not all dogs are equally civilized, however. In my experience, there are two types of dogs. The first is a normal dog that thinks and behaves like a typical lab. The second is the evolved dog, who is extremely intelligent and thinks and behaves more like a human than a dog.

The less evolved dogs, i.e., the vast majority, believe that humans are essentially big furless versions of themselves. Reminiscent of their wolf ancestors, they are willing to accept humans as "pack leaders" because they are able to provide the things that dogs want, such as protection, food, and affection. In return, they follow and offer more or less unconditional love and loyalty. To most dogs, humans are so smart they are almost magical. Food appears every night, there is a house that is warm and secure, it has always been there and always will be there, and the people in the house care about them and how they feel. These dogs pay close attention to their owner's needs. They obsess about accurately reading body language, facial expressions, and tone of voice.

These kinds of dogs will do just about anything their owner wishes and provide for his every need. These dogs make excellent pets and special assistants to the physically impaired. Like a member of a wolf pack, they do not question their leader. Mr. Wolfman's idea that dogs should think of their owners as "gods" is based on this type of dog.

The reason these dogs disobey is not because they intend to but because they don't fully understand their owner's wishes. For example, the owner comes home at night after a long day at work. The dog hears her drive up or put the key into the door and gets excited. When the door opens he runs to the door and jumps up with excitement. The owner has on a new dress or stockings and doesn't want the dog to jump up that particular night. She says "no" and "down," but most dogs can't pick up on the subtleties of when its okay to jump up and when it's not. In the primitive wolf pack, certain behavior is okay or it isn't-if nothing else there's clarity.

Clarity is what most dogs need from humans. Without clear direction from humans, they get confused. And they can get frustrated and take that frustration out on other dogs. (That's one reason I am very careful in approaching strange dogs. You never know how stable they are or how they will behave.)

A few dogs have evolved beyond the common wolf-dog mentality. I am one of them. I am different from other dogs because I not only understand human emotions and body language, I understand their actual words and act appropriately.

I don't need M&D to provide leadership. I can provide my own leadership, thank you very much. Most dogs follow along when their owners go for a walk. They are just happy to be with them. I understand that the walks are intended for the dog, not the owner. It shouldn't seem unusual, then, that I go on walks when I want to go and I walk where I want to walk. I'm not spoiled. I'm smart.

When I'm home I have my security duties, and I perform them whether or not M&D are there or are watching. In the car, I navigate no matter who is driving. No one has to ask.

If most dogs are like privates in an army ruled by human generals, I am a colonel in that army. The generals determine the overall battle plan, relying on the colonels' leadership and judgment to carry it out. The privates do what the colonels order, and the generals depend on the colonels to know what orders to give. Everyone knows that the colonels run the army. The difference is that in the world of dogs, most privates aren't smart enough to know a colonel when they see her.

BOOK THREE

THE END OR THE BEGINNING?

Book three is about the last years of my life.
I introduce the reader to Rushie Rule 10, my
final rule. I also find that as I go through
life, sometimes it is the simple pleasures
that matter most. I describe my increasingly
poor health and how I bravely face death.
Sometimes, death is more difficult for the
loved ones than it is for the dying, as was
true for my family and me.

Diary: *November 19, 2002.* Rushie suddenly is hard of hearing. It happened almost overnight. I read that deafness is common among predominantly white fox terriers, but I never thought it would happen to our Rushie. She's only 11 years old—late middle age in dog years. Plus, I keep her in great physical condition by throwing her toy every night. She's as trim and fit as ever. I thought regular exercise would keep her young (as I secretly hope it will do for me). So much for my fountain-of-youth-through-exercise theory.

Rushie: Losing my hearing was the weirdest
thing. It happened so fast. It seemed like one
day I could hear and the next day I couldn't.
I woke up one morning and felt like I was getting another ear infection. I wasn't concerned
about that-I'd gotten these infections many
times before-what concerned me was that this
time I couldn't hear. M told me breakfast was
ready but I didn't hear her until I looked up
and noticed her mouth moving. I walked closer
but still couldn't hear. When I saw that she'd
put my breakfast out, I figured that's what
she must have been telling me.

Things seemed pretty quiet that day while I

was guarding the house. I didn't hear any dogs bark, and the mail carrier drove up and left a package at the front door without making a sound. I'd have missed her entirely if I hadn't looked up just as she was getting back into her car. By then it seemed pointless to bark.

That evening we went for a walk. Everything seemed normal until I looked behind me and was shocked to see that a dog was right on my heels, not more than five feet away. I hadn't even heard him! Well, I didn't want that to happen again, so every few minutes I looked over my shoulder to make sure no one was back there.

A week or so later M took me to the vet. He gave me some medicine, and after a few days my hearing got better. I thought I was going to be okay. Then it got worse. This happened several times. Each time my hearing got better it was never as good as the time before and each time it got worse it was worse than the time before. After a year I couldn't hear much of anything, even on a good day.

I've learned to adapt. Thank goodness my eyes are still good. I can still guard the house, and I can read lips. This wasn't intentional. As my hearing declined, I found myself looking more and more closely at M&D's lips as they talked. After a while I could tell what they were saying by how their lips moved. It helped a lot.

Going deaf isn't all-bad. I enjoy the peace

and quiet. I sleep more soundly than I ever have. When I could hear I always woke up when I heard the slightest noise. I never did like the sound of the TV or the radio in the background. Now I don't have to listen to them. I figure that there's not much I can do about my hearing, so I might as well adapt and get on with my life. I'd rather be able to hear, but I can't. What good does it do to mope around feeling sorry for myself?

* * * * * * *

Let's see. D's last entry was written November 19, 2002, and the next one is August 1, 2004. Apparently, I didn't do anything worth writing about in two and a half years! Let me fill you in on what happened.

For one thing, D spent a lot of time at work. He said there were issues relating to accreditation that needed to be addressed. In addition, because there had been state budget cuts, he needed to spend a lot of the time with alumni and business community leaders raising money. He still enjoyed his job, but was spending a lot more time doing it. M took a part-time teaching position and spent a lot of time at the university.

The result was that I had sole responsibility for the house most weekdays. I'd get up early and be at my post guarding the house by 7:30 a.m., Monday through Friday. I didn't take bathroom breaks. And because my hearing was so poor I had to rely on my eyes to spot intruders and couldn't take naps. It was a grueling schedule, and as I expected, my diligence was pretty much taken for granted.

Not to say that there weren't benefits. When everyone finally got home in the evening, we were content just to be around each other eating dinner and watching TV or reading. We didn't let the stress of work make us irritable and argumentative, and we relied on each other for comfort and support.

Plus, our hectic weekday schedule made weekend activities even more enjoyable. Anticipating trips to the cabin or the beach kept us motivated. During the week, playing the ring toy game with D and taking short walks with M became more enjoyable because our time together was so limited.

I worked hard, but enjoyed this period of my life, although I did notice my energy level was declining and my allergies were bothering me more. Also, by summer 2004 I was almost totally deaf.

Then, out of the blue, D decided to take another job in another city. A big change. And I wasn't even consulted.

Diary: *August 1, 2004.* We are moving to Northridge, which is in the northwestern part of the San Fernando Valley. Both Natalie and I wonder how it will affect Rushie–she didn't like the move to Fresno, and now that she's getting older she might be even less excited about this move.

Rushie: I wasn't happy at all when I realized that we were going to move again. Fresno wasn't my favorite place, but it was home. I liked our house and enjoyed walking around the neighborhood. I especially liked the fact that we could get to the cabin in less than an hour and that we went there often.

I knew something was happening when one day D packed his things and put them into his car. Clothes and stuff were piled everywhere, with no room for M or me. I wondered where he possibly could be going without us. He gave M and me a big kiss and hug and drove off. For a long time after that I saw him only on the weekends. We had fun when he came home, things would almost get back to normal, and he would leave again.

After several months of this, we packed our things and moved to Northridge.

When the movers came this time, I didn't get as upset as when they came in Spokane. I knew what to expect, which is not to say that I liked it. I don't think I'll ever get used to strangers coming in my house and taking my furniture. It just doesn't seem right.

The thing I like best about Northridge is the weather. It's quite a bit cooler than Fresno. There's also a nice park close to where we live with a trail that runs through it. M and I walk in the park quite often. Sometimes we walk to a shopping center nearby. I like that walk because I get to window shop, meet people, and go into the pet store. The thing is that although I enjoy going outside, I get tired so easily. My itching seems to be getting worse as well.

The house we moved into is nice enough, but at first I didn't know what to do with myself. I couldn't see out of the windows. It was a security nightmare. I'd get up in the morning ready to go to work, with nothing to do. It was frustrating and depressing-like forced retirement. Finally, M moved the sofa in front of the den window. I could get up on the back of the sofa and see everything in front of the house, from the front porch to the street. I went to work immediately. To spend my whole life in the security business and suddenly be forced into retirement was depressing, and I was happy to be working again. It is a good thing, too, because there are a lot of suspicious-looking people, dogs, and cars in front of our house. When I see them, I let them know in no uncertain terms that I am watching their every move. So far, we've had no trouble.

After several months, we moved again, not far away from where we were already living. I didn't get concerned about the move this time because D was there the whole time supervising. Plus, I'm getting used to this nomadic life (which is not to say I like it).

The house we moved into has a big deck that overlooks the canyon and the trail we walk along. The view reminds me of the cabin. The front of the house is gated and is fairly secure, so I mostly guard the back of the house. I watch people and dogs walk along the trail and bark if they get too close. I remain vigilant, but this seems like a pretty safe neighborhood.

I really thought my skin problem would improve when I left Fresno. It hasn't. Maybe it's because I've been nervous about all our moves. Maybe it's age. I'm not sure.

Diary: *October 27, 2004.* I wish we could do something about Rushie's skin problems. The vet is at a loss. Rushie goes through a regular syndrome. She gets itchy spots, which she scratches and licks until the fur is gone and the bare skin is raw. Infection inevitably follows. Then we take her to the vet. He gives her antibiotics and prednisone. This helps for a month or two, but then the cycle starts again. Even when she's not scratching, her coat isn't as shiny as it once was. Poor girl.

Rushie: Sadly, I'm really starting to feel my age. When I get itchy I get sick and don't feel like doing anything but sleeping. I hate going to the vet, although I admit he does make me feel better, at least for a while. But even at my best, I don't have the energy I once had. The only time I feel like my old self is when we go to the cabin and play in the snow. Lately when I see myself in the mirror I can't believe how old and haggard I look.

The first six months in Northridge were tough for me. I didn't feel good and had no energy. I don't think D realized how sick I was.

Diary: *January 10, 2005.* Moving from Fresno to Northridge has really disrupted Rushie's life. If anything, her itching is worse than ever. I realized this when Natalie made an emergency trip to Utah when her mother had surgery and left Rushie home with me.

Poor Rushie was home alone most of the day. I'd leave about 7:30 a.m. and come home at noon to let her out. I'd leave again at 1:00 p.m. and not get home at night until 7:00 p.m. This only lasted for a week, but by the end, I noticed how slowly she moved and how itchy she was. She woke me up one night to let her outside, and I saw that one eye was almost swollen shut and she had a dried, crusty residue on the sides of her mouth.

Natalie took her to the vet when she got home the next day. The blood tests showed that she had a severe infection caused by her scratching. The vet gave her antibiotics and prednisone, and this time kept her on the prednisone for an extended period. She got better right away and continued to improve until she was almost her old self. Her coat grew out, we got her trimmed, and she seemed like she was feeling better. I notice, however, that because of the prednisone she's putting on some weight for the first time in her life. There's another anomaly in her blood that the vet can't seem to figure out. The vet in Fresno told us the same thing just before we left. They both said not to worry, just wait and see what happens.

Rushie: I was never so miserable in all my life as when I first moved to Northridge. I felt exhausted from the time I got up in the morning until I went to bed at night. I wanted to sleep all the time. Whenever I was awake I wanted to scratch, but scratching made me itch even more. I finally got so tired that I could barely scratch, even though I itched like crazy. Sometimes when I slept I would have one of my favorite dreams and wake up feeling happy. Then, when I got up, my joints would hurt, and I'd feel dizzy. All I wanted to do was to fall asleep again and hope for a good dream.

D took me for a walk one evening when M was gone, but after walking only a couple of blocks I felt so tired I knew I just couldn't make it. I tried to turn around, but D wouldn't let me. I sat down, but D just kept pulling on my leash. There was nothing I could do. It was like a forced march. D was possessed. Finally, after what seemed like eternity, we came to the road at the top of the canyon that led down hill back to our house. I was so relieved to be going home again.

I could tell that D was mad at me for not wanting to walk, but I was so tired by the time I got home that all I could do was get up on the couch and go to sleep. That night I dreamed I that was young again running across the meadow with all of the dogs following me. When I got to the lake and started to swim I noticed that all of the itching was gone. When I woke up in the morning I was happy until I realized that feeling good was just a dream.

Still, I enjoyed life. As I got less active, I began to appreciate the simpler pleasures in life, like going to the store with D.

Diary: *February 12, 2005.* Rushie can be so endearing. Maybe it is because she is so sparing with her affection that when she does show some it means more. She sleeps with us at night, but at the foot of the bed. When we reach down to pet her she acknowledges our affection with a low guurrr. Very occasionally she rests her chin on one of our legs. When she does, neither of us moves, and we savor the moment.

Although she's not fond of touching, she demonstrates her affection in other ways.

I recall one time when I took my son on a camping trip to visit the north side of the Grand Canyon and Zion and Bryce National Parks. Freddy was eight years old; it was the first time just the two of us went on a vacation together. Father and son bonding time was my plan.

It was about three years after his mother and I separated, and because I lived in LA and she in Seattle, I savored the summers I spent with him. This special vacation would be a time for us to really connect. As we drove north on I-15, we talked, which wasn't hard, because Freddy has always been a talker. On this trip he filled every pause in the conversation with questions. "Dad, how big is the Grand Canyon?" "Dad, will we be able to ride horses?" As he looked at the brochure about Bryce Canyon, "Dad, what makes the rocks red?"

I was thoroughly enjoying our Q&A session, even though I didn't have many answers, when Freddy became uncharacteristically quiet. I looked over at him belted securely in the front seat, and asked why he was so quiet. He looked up at me, his big brown eyes sparkling, and said, "I'm just thinking about how much fun we are going to have." He looked so cute with that little smile and the twinkle in his eyes that my heart melted. I thought, one day he's going to give some lucky girl that same look, and it will melt her heart too.

With Freddy's image seared in my memory, years later Rushie and I got in the car one night to pick up a pizza for dinner. She knew that we weren't going on a trip where she would be required to navigate, so she stayed in driving position only a minute or two and then got into the front passenger's seat and lay down. After getting settled, she looked up at me with her big brown eyes twinkling and gave me the same look Freddy had years before. My heart melted. I'm not sure when she started to give me this look, but now she does that almost every time she and I go to the store at night. And her loving look through those big brown eyes has the same effect. Every time.

Rushie: D's right. I'm not the touchy-feely type. But it doesn't mean that I don't care. I love M&D, and I know they love me. I don't need constant reassurance. I know who I am and I'm comfortable with it. I think that it is important to retain one's dignity.

A mistake that labs and a lot of other dogs make is to give unconditional love. I know, unconditional love is what many people find so endearing about dogs, but I think that most dogs give it because they are not smart enough to think for themselves. I heard about this dog (if I recall correctly, it was part lab) that was found near death on the doorstep of a house. A few days after they moved into the house, the couple heard scratching at the door. When the woman opened the door, she saw this poor dog lying on the doorstep, blood oozing from its head onto the doormat. She put the dog into the car and took him to the vet. The vet removed two, .22 caliber bullets. The nice couple nursed the dog back to health and adopted him. Later, they found out that the people who had lived in the house previously had taken the dog to the outskirts of town, shot him, and left him for dead. Apparently, they didn't want to take the dog with them when they moved. The poor dog didn't die and struggled for days to find his way home. When he did, fortunately for him, his old owners had already gone.

This pathetic tale of misplaced loyalty is exactly how many dogs would react if placed in a similar situation. Not me. I am an equal member of the household and expect to be treated appropriately. When M scolds me and I've done nothing wrong, I let her know by not talking to her for hours afterward. When I see her I give her a look that lets her know she was wrong. If I were ever in a situation in which my owners treated me even close to the way those people treated that poor lab (see, I can take pity even on a lab; no dog should be treated like that), I would never come back. Ever.

I am fortunate in that I am very attractive, smart, and an expert in household security. I could find another home easily. Most dogs aren't that lucky. But even if I weren't so fortunate, I would never, ever put up with abusive treatment. I respect myself too much.

I also believe that most dogs make the mistake of being too affectionate. It's simple economics: the more you supply kisses, hugs and cuddles, the less value they have. I love M&D, but I am careful not to devalue my affection by being too overt and demonstrative. For example, D talks about how one look from me can melt his heart. That's exactly what I intend. When we take a short drive at night to pick up a pizza or Chinese food I don't need to navigate, and after I make sure that we get onto the main road okay, I can relax and lie down on the front seat. I like these little trips with D and I tell him so with my eyes. He usually gives me a pat on the head in return. I know we have a special relationship. What good would it do for me to jump up on his lap and lick him in the face-to force my affection on him?

I realize that I express my love and friendship more subtly than most dogs. But I *do* express it. I recommend considered restraint as the key to a good relationship among equals. It works and it is dignified.

I've always tried to be a contributing member of the household. In addition to my regular jobs I help D with his work. But one time my willingness to help backfired.

Diary: *March 27, 2005*. Rushie gets the biggest kick out of going to work with me. I don't take her during work hours–that would be unprofessional–but sometimes I take her to the office at night or on the weekends. I do this often enough that she gets excited when I ask, "Rushie, would you like to go to work with me?"

When we get into the building I take her off the leash, and she charges around inspecting the hallways and any open office, much to the surprise of the occupant. After she explores the building she comes to my office and waits for me to finish. She waits patiently for 20 minutes or so, after which she bored and lets me know it's time to go.

One time I took her to work in Spokane. During her exploration she found an open door and let herself in. After looking around she sat down next to the desk. Just then the professor returned to her office to see Rushie sitting there looking at her as if to say, "I've been waiting. I was told to come here for advising." She knew who Rushie was and took her back to my office, laughing, saying that she didn't know I had admitted a new student. As it turned out, this was the same woman who nicknamed Natalie the "Dog Lady." I was sure that I'd now become the "Dog Dean."

Another time I took her to school with me in Fresno. She did her usual exploration of the hallways and then charged through the suite on her way to my office. What she saw next stopped her cold. First, she noticed that my secretary was there, which was unusual but not distressing. Then, my secretary's Doberman jumped out from behind the desk and issued a deep, challenging growl.

My assistant grabbed her dog and I grabbed mine. I carried Rushie into my office and shut the door. She sat there shocked (shocked!) that another dog was in her office. When my assistant and her dog left, I let Rushie out. She explored the office to make sure everything was okay and in particular that the Doberman who had invaded her territory was gone.

Rushie is cautious and never forgets. From then on, when I took her to the office, she explored it thoroughly to make sure there were no dangerous animals lurking behind the desks.

Last night I took her to my Northridge office. She was excited to see where I worked and thoroughly inspected the area. I noticed how much less energy she has now. She got tired walking up the stairs.

Rushie: I love going to work with D. We usually go at night because we both work during the day. D has an important job, with his own office, just like me. Because I'm the boss's daughter, I feel I have the right to go pretty much anywhere I want. People at work always know who I am.

The first thing I like to do is to look around the building and into each room. That time in Spokane, I was going down the hall when I saw that one of the office doors was open. I went inside to make sure everything was okay. Everything looked fine, but I thought I recognized a familiar smell, so I waited to find out who it belonged to. This nice lady came into the room, and I immediately recognized her as someone M had introduced me to. I said hello and made sure she was okay, and then took her to D's office. D laughed when she asked if I was enrolled as a student. I'd never thought about going to college before, but it seemed like it might be interesting. Then I started thinking about all my responsibilities and decided I just didn't have the time. Who would take care of M, much less provide security services, if I were at school all day? Best to leave college to Freddy, I thought.

After we moved to Fresno, D took me to work quite a few times. He had a nice building and a big suite of offices. I liked getting the chance to walk around the building before going to D's office and helping him with his work. Lots of times I solve very difficult problems for him. I don't mind helping, but don't like to waste too much time just sitting around his office. One time we were there for almost two hours, and I got pretty irritated. "I don't expect you to help me guard the house," I told him, "why should I spend so much time helping you do your work?" He didn't pay much attention, and I finally got up and sat in front of the door. I had had enough, and wanted to go home. He got the message.

The time that D's assistant brought her dog to work was really a surprise. It was also against the rules. Because D is the boss, and I am the boss's daughter, when I come to work with him, I don't expect to meet any other dogs, especially not in his office suite! This time there was this huge Doberman who actually growled at me, as if I were the one out of place. After setting him straight I went into the office with D. When we came out he was gone. Good thing, because I was still pretty mad.

I only went with D to his office in Northridge once. When we arrived, I was excited to see the building. We climbed up two flights of stairs to his office. By the time we got to the top, I was pretty tired. In my younger days, I thought, I wouldn't even have noticed the climb.

There were offices all around the outside of the building with an open space in the middle and an atrium below. I walked through the hallway that was between the atrium and the offices-there was no sign of other dogs, thank God-and finally went into the suite where D had his office.

It was really nice. I lay down on the carpet next to his desk while he worked. I tried to help, but I was so tired from the walk up the stairs that I fell asleep. Finally, we walked back to the car. I looked at the building as we left and wondered how many more times I'd get to go to work with D.

Lately it seems as if even the smallest exertion exhausts me.

Diary: *June 12. 2005.* Natalie's mom is having trouble recovering from the surgery she had last January. Natalie decided to stay with her for a couple of weeks to help her recuperate. On Sunday, she and Rushie left to visit "Grandma."

It's a long drive from LA to St. George–about eight hours–but

Rushie enjoyed the ride and was excited about visiting "grandma." She loves to visit relatives and friends and loves it even more if she gets to stay overnight. She has always liked her visits because Helen treats her like a granddaughter–and Rushie loves to be spoiled. Now that Helen lives in St. George, Rushie likes it even more because she has her own guesthouse.

The family has three houses on the same street. One is where Natalie's sister, Anne, lives. The other, right next door, is where Helen lives, and the third, at the end of the street, is the guesthouse. At night Rushie sleeps in the guesthouse and during the day she spends most of her time at Grandma's house being pampered.

Rushie: D's right. I love visiting Grandma West. The drive is nice, and there are lots of fields with cows and horses and hills and mountains to watch as we drive. M always gets excited when she sees cows and horses. Her eyes get wide and she says, "Look, Rushie! Horsie, horsie" or "cows" (pronounced, "couuws"). I always look at them and pretend that I'm interested. I'm not sure what the excitement is about. Horses and cows all look pretty much alike to me. But it seems to make her happy, so I play along, and it helps pass the time.

I know we are going on a long trip when M&D put their suitcases in the car. They usually tell me where we are going so I am prepared. Sometimes, it is a bit confusing when they say we are going to "Grandma's" and don't tell me which one. Once we leave I know as soon as we get to the highway which grandma we are visiting–North is to visit Grandma Evans and South is to visit Grandma West.

When we got to the freeway and headed south, I knew that we were going to see Grandma West. (Interesting, isn't it, that we drive south, then east, then north to visit Grandma West.) This trip was a bit weird because D stayed home and M and I took the trip alone. At first I missed D but after a while I realized how nice it was to be on a "girls only" trip. Also, M talks to me while we're driving, whereas D is usually pretty quiet.

Grandma West gives me snacks and lets me do pretty much what I want. Any time I want to go into the back yard she opens the door. Most of the time when we are alone she reads or watches TV and I sleep on the sofa. In the old days I'd be bored just sitting around. But now I don't mind not doing much for a few hours.

One of the best things about where Grandma lives now is that she has two houses. One is the guesthouse where we sleep. It's nice, with lots of rooms and a big back yard. I have this house pretty much to myself, so it's a good place to relax and not be bothered by kids or dogs. The other is where she lives. I like this arrangement. I spend the nights at the guesthouse and the days at Grandma's house.

On the drive up M told me that Grandma was feeling pretty weak and would need help to re-gain her strength. The doctor told her she should walk twice a day. The problem was that she didn't have a lot of energy and wouldn't take her walks like the doctor ordered. I'd wake up from a nap and try to get her to go for a walk, but she'd just sit there and read or watch TV. M would try to get her to walk, but she'd just smile and say, "maybe later." Finally, after M practically begged her to go for a walk, she said okay. She got up and went into the garage-which I thought was pretty strange place to start a walk.

That's when I saw the wheelchair.

At first I didn't pay much attention, but when Grandma grabbed the handles and started to push it out to the street, I thought that it might take her mind off her exercise if I hopped up on to the seat and kept her company. So I did, and it worked.

From then on, once or twice a day I'd go to the garage and hop into the wheelchair, hoping that Grandma would take the hint and go for a walk. (M thought I did this just so I could get a ride, but I was only trying to help.) My strategy worked. The whole time I was there, we walked every day, twice most days. By the time I left Grandma was feeling better and was getting stronger.

I'm a good granddaughter.

I felt pretty good when we were visiting Grandma. I think that helping her took my mind off my own problems. Now that I'm back home, I'm feeling worse than ever.

MY LIFE BY RUSHIE, BY FRED EVANS * 199

Diary: *July 8, 2006.* Rushie's health continues to decline. She sleeps virtually all day and all night. She can't hear anything anymore. But amazingly enough she seems to be able to read lips and has learned sign language. If her back is to me and I call her name I get no response. If she's looking at me and I say, "Rushie come." She does. She also does her tricks by watching hand signals. We didn't teach her. She picked it up on her own.

As weak as she is, she is still the same Rushie with a very strong independent streak. Sometimes, Natalie and I will look at her lying there sleeping and just want to hug and pet her and tell her that everything is going to be okay. When we do, Rushie endures for a minute or two, and then growls to let us know that enough is enough.

We took her to the dreaded vet a week ago. He took an x-ray and another blood test. He called last night and told Natalie that Rushie has a tumor in her stomach and that her blood test indicated it might be cancer. He said he couldn't treat her but gave us the name of a specialist. I called his office and was told that the operation to remove the tumor would cost $3,500. Natalie and I are trying to decide whether to have the surgery. The money isn't an issue. The problem is that they can't know whether the tumor is malignant or not until they operate and if it is they have no way of predicting whether the surgery will be a success. We hate to put her through the pain and trauma of surgery for nothing. We don't know what to do.

Rushie: I don't want to have surgery. I hate going to the vet's. I hate the smell of hospitals and sick animals. Please don't make me have surgery!

I feel weak all the time. I don't have any energy. I've always been a good sleeper, but lately I've slept so soundly I don't even dream. I sleep for hours without moving. When

I finally wake up I'm so stiff I can hardly walk.

What I miss most are the dreams. I love my dreams and always feel good when I wake up after having one. I haven't had one of my dreams for months now.

As sick as I am, I still go to work every morning and guard the house. I'm wondering how much longer I can do this, however. Every morning it gets harder and harder. Too bad I don't have a daughter or son to take over the security duties and give me more time to rest.

In this next entry D is surprised that I lost my temper. Why is he so surprised?

Diary: *August 15, 2005.* Sometimes, Rushie seems almost human. Last night, she joined me in bed for her pig's ear (she demands her treat at 10:00 P. M. sharp and doesn't like it to be late). I was in bed reading, and she was at the foot of the bed working on her "piggy." After she finished, she went to her water bowl in the bathroom to get a drink.

While in the bathroom, she decided to lie on the throw rug in front of the sink. Being the fastidious dog she is, she couldn't do this without rearranging the rug. With one paw, then the other she scratched and pulled to make the rug more comfortable. But the more she scratched and pulled the more bunched up and uncomfortable it became. Finally, after she worked on the rug for several minutes, I heard a snort, and she took both feet and pulled the rug into a lump and stalked off. I thought to myself, "Temper, temper."

Rushie: Okay. Maybe I did lose my temper, but so do you. How many times have you done a chore for M—drilling a hole in the wall to

hang a picture or putting furniture together-
when things didn't go as you planned and you
got mad? Getting mad at the rug isn't much
different than that, is it?

Plus, you've done lots of other silly things.
Remember the time you went to the wrong funeral? It was in Fresno and you decided to attend the funeral of a retired faculty member
you had never met. You were early for a change
and went to the spot where you had been told
the services were to be held. There were two
services being held at the same time and you
went to the wrong one. You even talked to a
grieving relative, telling him what a fine man
he was and what a good reputation he had among
the faculty. The person just smiled and nod-
ded. Only later did you find out that you were
at the wrong memorial service. That's silly! I
would never make a mistake like that.

After I got a drink, I looked at the rug and
thought it might be a good place to sleep. The
problem was that there was a fold in the middle that would make the bed lumpy. I tried to
straighten it out, but the more I tried the
worse it got. I finally gave up in disgust.
Some things are just not worth the effort.

Not feeling well is taking its toll.

Diary: *September 1, 2005.* Rushie's been getting more and more
lethargic. She refuses to go on long walks any more. She sleeps all
day. And she is almost totally deaf. She is 13 years old now, so
maybe its just age catching up with her.

The last time we went to the cabin, Rushie stayed awake the whole four-hour ride, and when we got there she checked out her yard and the deck. Then she curled up on the sofa and went to sleep, waking only long enough to have dinner. After eating she went into the bedroom, hopped up on the bed and didn't even come out for snacks when we ate.

She slept through the night and didn't get out of bed until breakfast was on the table. When we finished she went back to bed and slept until afternoon. She seemed to feel better and wanted to go outside. I threw her toy, but she tired quickly and wanted to go back inside. Only a couple of years ago she would have played that game until I got tired.

Once inside, Rushie jumped up on the couch and slept until dinner.

Poor thing is running out of energy.

Rushie. My energy level is way down. I've never been big on walks, because, as I've explained, I don't like being led. But occasional walks with M are enjoyable if I lead. At our current house in Northridge I like to take her to the shopping center where I can see people, window shop, and walk through the pet store. Lately, I haven't even had the energy to do that.

I haven't been getting much exercise lately because I've been concentrating on finishing the book, and after I work on it for a while, I don't have the energy to do much else. I hardly ever take M for a walk anymore. I feel guilty because I know she enjoys it, but I'm just too tired.

The other day I saw M putting on her walking shoes. I was feeling pretty good about the progress I made on the book and thought I'd go with her. Walking to the shopping center, meeting new people and window-shopping seemed like a perfect diversion. After only two blocks I realized that I just didn't have enough energy for even a short walk. I turned around and took M back to the house. I could tell she was disappointed.

After we got back to the house, I lay there thinking how pathetic it was to tire so easily.

Later that evening I felt better after looking at myself in the mirror. I still looked good. Maybe a little heavier than I once was, with more white hair, but I still have a pretty face and the big, brown eyes that everyone loves.

Fortunately, I'm never too tired for a party. This year we had a good one, with lots of people.

Diary: *January 8, 2006.* We had our Twelfth Day of Christmas party last night. It was a great get-together. Rushie was like her old self, greeting the guests and being a good hostess. She loves to have people in the house and the more the better as far as she's concerned.

Rushie: I'm making good progress on my book and am current on the diary entries, so when I realized that M&D were having a party, I got pretty excited. I love entertaining, seeing old friends and meeting new people. M&D know lots of interesting people, and I do my best to make sure everyone feels welcome.

This was one of our best parties ever. Our small house was full of people, and everyone was laughing and talking and having a good time. I did my usual hostess thing and welcomed each of the guests individually. Everyone smiled and said what a cute and well-behaved dog I was, so I knew that I was doing a good job.

When the food was served a few of the guests began giving me treats. I could tell from their faces and my sampling that M did a good job preparing the food. I especially liked the roast beef. I saw D sitting on a chair with his plate on his lap eating and talking. I walked up to see how he was doing, thinking he might share some of his food. Sure enough, when he saw me he gave me a big bite of delicious roast beef.

I must have eaten too much that night because the next day I was nauseous. I couldn't eat anything the next morning, and about ten o'clock I went outside and threw up in the bushes. I felt completely drained-absolutely no energy-and slept all day. I could eat only a few bites of dinner that night and went to bed right after eating.

I've recovered a bit since then-my appetite's come back, but I still don't have any energy. Last evening I went outside with D and walked around the pool area-something I wouldn't even have considered a walk a year ago-but was exhausted when I got back to the house. I can tell that M&D are concerned about me because they are being exceptionally nice. M even carried me up the stairs last night. I told her she didn't need to do that, but it was very thoughtful of her.

Oh, I almost forgot. For the last month or so I've been so weak that I haven't been able to get up on the bed by myself. Someone has to lift me. One evening about a week ago I was feeling pretty good, and without thinking I ran into the bedroom and tried to jump up on the bed. Well, I jumped, but not much happened. My front feet barely reached the top of the bed, my chest crashed into the mattress, and I fell flat on my back on the floor. It didn't hurt, but it was humiliating. M had to pick me up and put me on to the bed like a puppy.

I've been so tired lately; all I've been able to do is sleep.

Diary: *January 25, 2006.* We took Rushie to the vet today and he confirmed that the tumor was malignant and had spread to her liver. He said she had a month to live, maybe less. Natalie cried and held Rushie close to her all the way home.

We wondered if we made the right decision by not having surgery. Ultimately, we decided that the very uncertain benefit of surgery wasn't worth the trauma it would cause Rushie. Now we are second-guessing that decision.

My biggest fear is that Rushie will be in pain. I remember that my father passed away from cancer of the liver. He was in a great deal of pain and went in and out of consciousness his last week. I didn't want that to happen to Rushie. I asked the vet if he would come to our house if we had to put her to sleep. I didn't want her last thought to be going to the dreaded vet's office. Neither could I bear the thought of her dying in pain.

I woke up about 2:00 a.m. last night and looked at Rushie sleeping at the foot of the bed. I dreamed she was miraculously cured and back to her old, energetic self. She was so still that I couldn't resist touching her to see if she was still breathing. She was. Then I noticed the twitching of the legs and the little yips that told me she was dreaming. I couldn't know for sure, but she seemed to be having a happy dream, and when she woke up she acted like she felt better.

It is so sad to know she is dying. My throat closes and my eyes water every time I think about losing her. Natalie is depressed all the time. I just hope that Rushie isn't in pain. It might be easier for her than it is for us because she doesn't know she's dying.

Rushie: You don't think I know I'm dying? Of course I do! Dogs know that death is part of the cycle of life. We do not, I do not, fear death. I am grateful for having lived a full life. I am blessed to be beautiful and intelligent. I have a wonderful family, I've visited many places and hiked the most interesting trails. D taught me to drive when I was a puppy, and I became an excellent navigator. As security chief, I have saved our family from many intruders. I learned English and am completing the first ever autobiography written by a dog. I've been a good family member and companion. I've accomplished a lot in my lifetime, I'm pleased to say.

How interesting is life? Just when you think it's about over you learn something new! I realized there was a rule I've lived by for most of my life, but never expressed. It is **Rushie Rule 10.** *Do your best and never have regrets.*

Mistakes are part of life. Acknowledge your mistakes, learn from them, and move on. If you make a mistake after doing your best, don't feel guilty. It's when you haven't tried hard enough that guilt is deserved. If you do your best, your conscience will be clear.

I've worked hard. Although I've made mistakes, I've corrected them. I've done my best. I am ready for whatever is next.

I don't know what will happen when I die. People say that animals don't have souls. Maybe. Maybe not. Then again, maybe people don't have souls either. After death may come darkness, or possibly something more.

I don't worry about death. I welcome it. One good thing about dying is that I won't have to make another trip to the vet's!

Speaking of my health, I've been feeling better ever since I began dreaming again. It is my favorite dream where I run across the fields, my paws barely touching the ground, with all of the other dogs trying to catch up. I swim across the lake to M&D. But instead of getting in the car with them, I get in the car by myself and begin to drive off. I look out the window and see them waving and smiling. As I look more closely, I see that M has tears running down her cheeks. I stop the car, get out, and give her one last hug. I get back in the car and drive down the road. I don't know where the road leads, but I have a full tank of gas and I can't wait to see what is around the next turn.

As I drive down the road, I see that it is a beautiful, sunny day. The window is open and the cool air is blowing on my face. There are trees on one side of the road and a meadow with horses and cows on the other. As I pass, I think about how much M would enjoy seeing them and how she would say excitedly, "Look, Rushie! Horsie. Cow." Up ahead the road turns and I can't wait to see what's around the corner. I know it will be interesting and exciting. But just before I get to the corner I wake up. In the morning I feel refreshed and optimistic. I know that one day soon I will be able to see what's around the corner.

Diary: *January 30, 2006.* Miraculously, Rushie seems to be feeling better. She doesn't act like she is in pain. She's eating better and sleeping less. Every morning she gets up and goes to work guarding the house. Last weekend we decided to take advantage of her sprightliness and go to the cabin for the weekend.

We left early Friday afternoon. Rushie was excited when we told her we were going to the cabin-in-the-woods. She supervised as I packed the car, and we both got impatient as we waited while Natalie watered the plants.

Rushie navigated the entire trip. The next day, instead of lapsing into an exhausted sleep, she actually wanted to go outside and play in the snow. I had fun throwing snowballs and she had fun chasing them. When I brought Rushie back into the cabin snowy and wet, Natalie wrapped her in a towel and sat with her in front of the fireplace. As I watched Natalie hold Rushie lovingly in her arms, the crackling fire warming her, I thought about how much joy that little bundle of fur had given us.

The remainder of the weekend saw Rushie at her energetic best. We both told ourselves, without really believing it, that maybe Rushie wasn't so sick after all. I brought the video camera to the cabin to record some of the happy times. Regrettably, I never got around to using it.

Rushie: I've been feeling much better the last

few days. For a while I had a sharp pain in my stomach that would come and go several times a day and wake me up at night. Lately I haven't felt that pain, and I've been sleeping better. The best part is that every night I've been having the dream where I drive the car. Each time it seems like I get closer and closer to seeing what's around the next turn. In the morning I wake up refreshed and excited about what is to come. I know things will be different soon, so I want to take advantage of all that this life has to offer now.

That's why I was so happy to go to the cabin. We hadn't gone there for a long time, and I really missed it. One of the bad things about living in Northridge is that we don't go there as often as when we lived in Fresno.

D asked if I wanted to go to the cabin as soon as we got up in the morning. I think I was pretty clear that I wanted to go, but it seemed to take forever for M&D to shower, eat breakfast, pack their bags, and load the car. Once the car was packed, I figured they were about ready to go, but I was wrong. More things to do, apparently. I waited and waited, trying to be patient. When D opened the car door and lifted me up on the seat I figured we were finally going to leave, so I got into driving position. Well, I stood there-and stood there-all by myself. No one else got in the car for what seemed like forever. As it turned out, D was waiting for M, who was watering her plants while imitating the world's slowest gardener.

Finally, D got in, started the engine, and backed the car out of the garage. After a few minutes M hopped in and we drove off. It felt good to get on the road and I was excited to be going to the cabin. After an hour or so, when I knew that D was going in the right direction, I got into M's lap to settle down and take a short nap. But I couldn't sleep, so I hopped up and looked out the window while M looked for cows. I could smell the fresh air and pine trees as we finally began the steep climb up the mountain. As we got closer to the cabin I could see there was snow on the ground and knew I'd get a chance to play in it. I love winter sports, like chasing snowballs and jumping into snowdrifts. I've driven with D to where he skis and once, I even rode up on a ski lift. But I've only skied with D once. Maybe someday I'll get another chance.

When we got to the cabin I went through my usual routine of checking inside and outside for intruders and possible danger. As I am sure you now understand, this is a very important job. M&D aren't as security conscious as I am; it doesn't bother me, I know what needs to be done.

After he unpacked and lit a fire, D and I went outside to play. D threw snowballs and I chased them. It's a simple game, but I like it. In the old days I could chase snowballs all day. This time I lasted 15 minutes or so. At least it was long enough to get snowy and wet. When we went back into the cabin I knew M would be there with a towel to dry me off and a blanket to keep me warm. We sat by the fire, and I relaxed and enjoyed the evening.

The next morning I got up bright and early, went outside to look around and go to the bathroom. All was well. No animals had dared come onto my property. D left for skiing, and M and I lounged around the cabin after breakfast. Right after lunch, we took a short walk, and I was able to make sure everything was in its place. (One time they cut down a big tree without telling me. I was pretty upset when I found out it was gone. The security chief should always be informed about these things before they happen!)

After D came back from skiing, we went outside and he threw snowballs into the ravine. I was okay going down the hill, but had a pretty hard coming back up—my feet sank into the snow as I struggled to climb the hill. Still, I had a lot of fun.

Sunday morning was a repeat of Saturday, I got up early, I felt good, had a walk, and played. That afternoon, we packed up the car and headed back home. I always hate leaving the cabin, but I knew it was time to go. I stood on the porch until M&D were in the car with the engine running. As I walked slowly to join them, I took one last look and thought how lucky I was to have this wonderful hideaway. On the drive home, I wondered how many more times I'd get to visit our cabin-in-the-woods.

Diary: *February 5, 2006.* Rushie's been doing great lately. It's been almost a month since the vet predicted she had only a month to live. I'm sure she has longer, maybe a lot longer. I had planned a ski trip to Utah with my son, but intended not to go if Rushie was getting worse. If anything she seems to be getting better. I called Freddy and told him I'd meet him in Salt Lake City. We plan to stay three nights and ski four days. I'm really looking forward to the trip.

Natalie and Rushie took me to the airport. As always, Rushie was excited about seeing me off. I said goodbye and hugged them both.

Rushie: Don't worry D, I feel pretty good. M and I will be okay. I've had more energy lately. Each morning I wake up refreshed and ready for a new day. I can't explain it, but I have the feeling that soon I won't feel sick. I think my dreams are giving me energy. I've even been taking M on short walks lately.

Diary: *February 10, 2006.* Rushie's decline has been so hard for Natalie. Rushie is her baby. She loves her so much. When we first got Rushie she could barely stand to be away from her.

Once when we were living in Spokane and Rushie was about two years old, Natalie became convinced that in rummaging around in the garage, Rushie had eaten snail bait. She called me at work and asked me what I thought. I listened to her story and the total lack of evidence that anything of the sort had happened and suggested that she not worry. When she called again, even more anxious, I told her to call the vet. The vet said she probably didn't need to worry but that he could pump Rushie's stomach if she insisted. Natalie rushed her to the vet to get her stomach pumped. The result? Rushie was traumatized and no snail bait was found. Natalie felt relieved and a bit silly. I asked her what she would do if it happened again. She said, "I'd have her stomach pumped!"

Most nights Natalie wakes up and checks to see if Rushie is breathing. She's done this since Rushie was a puppy. Now that Rushie is sick she checks her two or three times a night. Rushie's response is always the same: "Guurrr." Or, translated, "Leave me alone. Can't you see I'm trying to sleep?"

Rushie: I had that wonderful dream again last night. This time I was almost able to see what was around the curve in the road. The closer I got to the curve, the faster I drove. As I started the turn I thought I could see fields with snow-covered mountains on the other side. My heart was pounding. I woke up just as I was about to pass a grove of trees that obscured my view. I'd almost seen around the corner! I couldn't stop thinking about my dream and what was around that curve in the road.

I know I'll find out soon.

Diary: *February 15, 2006.* Freddy and I skied today. It snowed last night and we skied at Alta where they usually have the best powder. This time, however, the snow was wind-packed and heavy.

Rushie's condition is always in the back of my mind. It took the edge off the fun that Freddy and I usually have.

We drove to Park City for dinner after skiing. We didn't get back to the motel until late, so I didn't call to check on Rushie. I'm sure she's okay, though.

Diary: *February 20, 2006.* Rushie died in her sleep around 3:00 a.m. February 16, 2006. My cell phone rang in the middle of the night. By the time I realized it was ringing, it stopped, and I went back to sleep without checking the message.

The alarm jolted me awake at 7:00 a.m. The room was dark. The night before we had closed the heavy plastic-backed curtains specially designed to keep out the light of day. They did their job, I thought. Freddy was sleeping soundly, so I left the lights off and went into the bathroom to shave and shower.

When I finished I saw my cell phone lying on the nightstand and remembered that I'd had a call the night before. When I picked up the phone and saw there was a message I got a chill. It was from Natalie and what could it be but bad news about Rushie?

The message Natalie recorded at 3:20 a.m. said, "Fred. Rushie died. I just woke up to see how she's doing and she's dead. Call me back when you wake up."

I called immediately. She was in tears and could barely talk. The previous afternoon Rushie wanted to go outside. Natalie let her out, but instead of going to the bathroom and coming back inside, she went behind a bush and lay down. Natalie coaxed her back into the house. Several hours later she did the same thing. This time, Natalie had to carry her into the house. That evening she didn't eat and slept on the couch until bedtime.

About eleven, Natalie carried Rushie downstairs and laid her in her favorite spot at the foot of the bed. Worried, Natalie checked to see of Rushie was okay a couple of times before she went to sleep. She whispered in her ear, as she had many times over the last few days, "Don't worry, Rushie, you're going to heaven. Everything will be okay. You'll see."

After dozing off, Natalie woke at midnight and checked to see if Rushie was okay. She was sleeping soundly and breathing regularly. She gave her a pet and a hug. Rushie's response: "Guurrr." She checked again about 2:00 a.m. Rushie's legs were moving. She seemed to be dreaming.

At 3:15 a.m., she woke in a panic. She immediately checked Rushie. She put her hand on her stomach and couldn't feel her breathing. She shook her and said, "Rushie. Wake up!" No response. She knew Rushie was dead. But, she looked so comfortable, as if she were asleep. She couldn't believe that Rushie was dead, and kept hoping she would miraculously begin breathing. She called my cell phone.

No answer. She left a message. In sad futility, she petted and talked to Rushie, knowing it was over but desperately trying to deny the reality.

Eventually, she fell into a light sleep, and dreamed that Rushie woke up and was fine after all, a dream she's had every night since.

When I called that morning–it was one of those rare rainy and gloomy mornings in L.A.–Natalie told me she didn't have the heart to move Rushie; she looked so natural and comfortable lying at the foot of the bed. I told Natalie that I understood and cried with her on the phone. I told her that I would fly home immediately.

I arrived that afternoon. Natalie picked me up at the airport, tears in her eyes. As I put my bags into the car I thought, sadly, that this was the first time in years that Natalie had picked me up at an airport without bringing Rushie to greet me. Rushie liked to drive me to the airport and loved to pick me up and welcome me home. She'd always jump on my lap and nudge my ear with her nose. I realized that Rushie would never sit on my lap again.

Natalie and I didn't talk much. We were both lost in our own thoughts about Rushie. When we did try to talk we ended up crying.

I parked the car in the garage. As I walked to the front door I got a sinking feeling in the pit of my stomach. I knew that to see Rushie lying on the bed would make her death final in my mind.

I opened the door to the bedroom and was totally unprepared for what I saw. There was Rushie, lying at the foot of the bed looking for all the world like she was taking a nap. I went up to her and petted her side, half expecting a "Guurrr." But no sound came from her throat and no air from her lungs.

After procrastinating for a while, we called the vet. He said to bring her in, and he would have someone take care of the body. When I lifted her off the bed she was stiff, and seemed so light. She no longer looked like she was sleeping.

At the vet's an assistant solemnly ushered us in to an examination room where we put Rushie on the table. The vet came in and was very sympathetic. He told us that there was a company that would cremate her and give us the ashes. We liked the idea. He left us alone with Rushie. Both Natalie and I petted her and cried. I left after about ten minutes; Natalie stayed another fifteen, knowing that this would be the last time she would ever see her little Rushie.

Diary: *March 17, 2006*. It's been a month since Rushie died. We have her ashes in a nice velvet bag that says, "Until we meet at the Rainbow Bridge." We think of her every day. It is so lonely to come home from work, open the front door and not have Rushie run up, tail wagging, to welcome me. Dinner seems so solitary without her waiting close by (while pretending not to care) for a suitable offering of food.

We find ourselves reminiscing about her. Like the time Natalie tried a new brand of noodle casserole. I tried, like a good husband, to eat the dish. The first bite tasted unappetizing. By the second bite, I realized that the noodles were truly inedible. Natalie agreed. I thought Rushie might like it and offered her a noodle. She sniffed and politely but firmly refused. Even our dog thought the dish disgusting, we laughed.

Rushie's most distinctive personality trait was her inner direction. She knew whether she wanted to go for a walk, and if she went for a walk, where she wanted to go. She knew what games and toys she enjoyed. She was serious about her work and relentless about her morning guard duty. Once she made up her mind about something, there was no changing it. No matter how many toys we bought, the ring toy was the only one she wanted. Natalie got her an imitation bear rug to lie on at the cabin. She looked at it, walked over and peed on the bear's head and never went near it again. She loved people and liked to show off. With an appropriate audience she relished doing her tricks and reveled in the oohs and ahas and applause.

When Natalie first took Rushie to obedience school, the instructor said that we'd never be able to train her as long as we didn't deal with her "dominance issues." We never did. Not that we tried all that hard. We taught her tricks, but I would never say we trained her. More accurately, she transformed from a dominant dog to a contributing member of the family. She was never obedient, but she certainly accepted responsibility. She had her jobs (guarding and navigating) and her sports (the chasing games and swimming) and took them seriously.

Rushie was special and knew it. I am sure she believed that she had more in common with humans than dogs. Humans who didn't treat her as if she were special by telling her how cute and smart she was were scorned and ignored, as were dogs she couldn't dominate (that is, most dogs). She was relentless with cousin Trevor, satisfied only when he cowered in the corner at her slightest glance. Not surprisingly, Rushie had lots of human friends, and few dog friends. But I think she liked it that way.

Rushie was very refined. She didn't gulp her food or eat to excess. She also was extremely intelligent. She had a large English vocabulary. She always seemed to understand what was going on around her. Her intelligence helped to explain her affinity to humans and her ambivalence toward dogs.

She was a princess. She expected to be treated preferentially and was shocked when she wasn't. Although affectionate in her own way, she didn't like to be smothered. When I came home from work, she would walk up to say hello and let me scratch her ears, but would then return to what she was doing. It was as if to say, "Welcome home, D. Okay to pet me for a minute but don't get carried away. I have other pressing engagements." She loved the attention of strangers and visitors to our home. She was like the celebrity who is a challenge to relate to personally, yet revels in her adoring fans.

Having Rushie in our family was almost like having a very attractive, talented, but spoiled daughter. You love her to death and think she is wonderful, yet are frustrated by her rebellion and stubbornness. At the same time, you know the rebellion and stubbornness is part of what makes her unique. That was Rushie. Not a perfect dog. Not an obedient dog. But a wonderful and irreplaceable member of the family.

Diary: *December 10, 2006.* I haven't made a diary entry about Rushie for a long time now–almost a year. Today would have been her 15th birthday. We both really miss her–the house seems so empty and lifeless with her gone.

Lately, Natalie and I have been wondering if there is something like a Rainbow Bridge where dogs go after death, and if we will ever see her again. It would be nice, but the thought of life after death for a dog is probably just fantasy and wishful thinking. What I do know is that Rushie will always remain alive in our thoughts.

Rushie: Well, you got it partly right, D. Let me tell you what's going on.

When I went to sleep the night I died, I immediately began to dream. I ran across the fields, swam the lake, said goodbye to you and M, and drove off in the car, just like I had so many times before. This time, when I came to the curve in the road I didn't wake up, I just kept driving. I could finally see around the corner! I saw a beautiful meadow with green grass, butterflies, and birds. Beyond the meadow was a lake and beyond that snow-capped mountains. I stopped the car and got out to look. As I stood there thinking how beautiful it was, I began to hear voices in the breeze. The voices seemed to be calling me: "Rushie, come. Rushie, come." I looked around to see who was calling me, but no one was there.

As I turned to get back into the car, the voices began again. "Rushie, come. Rushie, come! We can run in the fields, swim in the lake, and hike in the mountains. We'll have fun. You'll see."

If there's one thing I've learned in all my years in the security business, it's to be careful. I am not inclined to trust voices in the wind. Still, there was something compelling and reassuring about what I heard. Should I take a chance, and follow the voices or should I get back in the car and drive? I decided to get back in the car. As I opened the door and got behind the wheel, I wondered where I would go. M&D weren't with me. I didn't know where the road led. I looked out at the meadow again. It was so appealing. I thought, "What would it hurt to explore for a few minutes?"

I cautiously walked into the meadow. The grass felt cool and moist on my feet. The smells were enchanting—I'd never experienced anything like them. As I walked further into the meadow I saw a group of dogs standing together, as if they were waiting for me. They seemed to be peaceful and content. I wasn't afraid and walked right up to them. One of them, a border collie, I think, said, "Rushie, we've been waiting for you. This is a wonderful place. The weather is perfect—it's never too hot—and there're lots of fun things to do."

I asked how long they had been there, but they

weren't sure. I gathered that the dogs come and stay for a while, but eventually leave. That seemed pretty strange to me. Another strange thing was that all of the dogs talking to me looked young and healthy. Their coats were shiny, and they were strong and energetic. None of them was old or weak. Except me. My fur was scraggly, and my joints hurt when I walked. I envied these youthful, strong dogs-they were like I used to be.

I asked them why they wanted me to stay. They said that although life in the meadow was good, they needed a leader-someone to teach them how to swim and show them the way to the mountains. I also learned that there were some dangerous animals, like mountain lions, wolves, and coyotes. They knew about my experience in the security business and said they would feel safer with me there to protect them.

Why not look around, I thought. I really didn't have any appointments, and if I got bored I could always go back to the car and continue driving. I told them that I would stay the night.

They were so happy. The border collie, named Jake, gave me a tour. He showed me where they slept and where they ate. "Luckily," Jake said, "we are just in time for dinner. And the food is wonderful." He doesn't know how discriminating my tastes are, I thought. I wasn't very hungry, but to be polite, I said I would try the food. After I took a small bite I realized that Jake was right. The food was delicious, as good as M's best!

After I'd eaten, I asked the dogs if they wanted to explore the meadow. They said yes and began to follow me. As I walked, I noticed that I felt strong and that my arthritis didn't bother me. So I began trotting then running. I felt like a puppy again. I ran and ran, with the other dogs following behind. We finally came to the lake. I stood on a rock overlooking the lake with the mountains in the distance. The water was as smooth as glass, not a ripple in sight. I looked down and saw my reflection. I couldn't believe what I saw. I was young again! I looked like I did when I was three or four years old. I had a perfect clip, and my fur was healthy and shiny.

It was then that I realized I could hear again. I could hear what Jake and the others were saying. I could even hear the beating wings of the butterflies as they flew by.

As I stood there trying to understand what had happened, I heard Jake say to the other dogs, "Isn't she beautiful? She's so strong and smart. I hope she'll stay with us." I looked down and told them I would stay, at least for a while. They were all relieved and happy.

So, M&D, don't worry about me. I am happy here. I've gotten the dogs organized and solved the problem they had with wolves.

As I learned, there are several wolves that live in the area and who would occasionally chase the dogs. Well, not long after I got here, a wolf saw me running through the meadow with all of the dogs following and thought it would be a good time to attack. He picked the wrong fox terrier. When I saw him coming I stopped dead in my tracks, instead of running as he expected. I then gave him a low, menacing growl to let him know I was deadly serious. When he stopped, I walked right up to him. We stood nose to nose and I told him that I would let him go this time, but if he ever came into our meadow again he would be very, very sorry. With a whimper he turned and scurried off, tail between his legs. Since that incident, we've had no more trouble with predators.

I've taught all of the dogs to swim, and we go to the lake almost every day. The water is clear and cool and refreshing. I've taken the dogs on expeditions to the mountains and taught them how to play in the snow. As fun as it is, I miss you not being there, D, to throw snowballs.

All of the dogs are nice, including one very well-behaved lab named Lukey. We've actually become good friends.

But I do miss you and M. I miss the fun we had together and being part of the family. I hope all is well with you and that someday we will be together again. I'd love to hop into the car and spend one more weekend at the cabin-in-the-woods.

THE END

APPENDIX ONE

RUSHIE RULES

If you've read my autobiography you've already know about my Rushie Rules. People ask me about the rules all the time because it helps them lead a better life. I've collected the rules below for easier reference. Some people keep the Rules on the nightstand beside their bed; others keep copies in their wallet or purse. One reader told me that she put a framed copy on her desk at work. Where (or if) you keep your copy is up to you. My only hope is that the Rules help you as much as they've helped me.

* * * * * * *

Rushie Rule 1: *Never gulp your food.* Taste first; make sure the food is fit to eat. Always eat slowly, leaving some food in the dish in case you get hungry later. Never overeat! Overeating can cause a stomachache and make you fat. As D says, obesity is a big problem in this country. Don't be a part of the problem!

Rushie Rule 2: *Communicate, communicate, communicate!* If something bothers you, say so. A good relationship requires open communication. Dogs are notorious for being doormats. Good dog/human relations require two-way communication-dogs should express themselves and humans should listen.

Rushie Rule 3: *Never do anything that you know is wrong.* Sometimes, people you like or even love will try to get you do something that you know in your heart is wrong. Don't be tempted! Part of growing up is developing a clear and honest understanding of right and wrong. Once you've developed that understanding, don't stray from it. Don't go jogging when you know it's wrong. Don't gulp your food, and never trust a lab.

Rushie Rule 4: *When you are right, stubbornness is a virtue.* Don't let others put doubts in your mind. And don't get discouraged if people (or dogs) don't understand. They don't get it and probably never will.

Rushie Rule 5: *Never lose your sense of humor.* I'm not a frivolous dog. I go to work and put my life on the line every day. In my work I see things that would make most individuals bitter and cynical. Every day people, dogs, and the occasional cat try to break into our home. I am the first and last line of defense for the entire family. Sometimes by the end of the day I am exhausted by my encounters. I could curl up in a ball and dwell on them and become bitter and angry. Instead, I happily greet D when he comes home and steal his napkin when he sits down to dinner. Humor helps me put the events of the day into perspective and helps me prepare for the difficult day ahead.

Rushie Rule 6: *Better safe than sorry.* Perhaps it is because I am in the security business, but I believe that caution is a virtue. Spontaneity has its place, but on the big issues in life try to minimize your risks by looking at the evidence carefully and not letting yourself get carried away by emotion.

Rushie Rule 7: *Never, ever trust a lab!* Labs slobber and knock things over and should never be let in the house. When they are outside they should always be on a leash. They are excessive eaters and should only be given dry food. I'm not being harsh. I'm being realistic. Some breeds need special treatment.

Rushie Rule 8. *To be good at anything worthwhile takes dedication and practice.* When you have a game or sport that you enjoy, stick with it. I play three sports-chasing the ring toy, chasing rocks and sticks, and chasing snowballs. Each has its own rules. I am very ethical. I follow the rules carefully and don't cheat. I don't change games. I am a perfectionist and want to be good at what I do.

Rushie Rule 9: *Nothing is too difficult if you apply yourself.* Keep trying. Take one step at a time, and before you know it, you've accomplished something big. If I can overcome my fear of water, you can overcome your fears as well.

Rushie Rule 10. Do your best and never have regrets. Mistakes are part of life. Acknowledge your mistakes, learn from them, and move on. If you make a mistake after doing your best, don't feel guilty. It's when you haven't tried hard enough that guilt is deserved. If you do your best, your conscience will be clear.

APPENDIX TWO

A LAYMAN'S GUIDE TO HOUSEHOLD SECURITY

I have worked in the security business for many years. Because I am familiar with every facet and nuance of household security, people naturally ask me what they can do to keep their home safe. As a public service, I offer here a five-step guide to better home security.

Step One. Choose your house or apartment carefully. There should be at least one window in the front of the house; it should offer a view of the front yard, including roads, driveways, walkways, and any other avenue of access. Avoid doors on the sides of the house, since they only provide additional opportunities for intruders. If you have a back yard, make sure it's fenced. Fences are a good deterrent and allow daytime security activities to focus on the front of the house.

Step Two. Get a reliable dog to stand guard. The dog must be intelligent, brave, committed, and large and strong enough to be a credible deterrent. A common error is to select large dogs, thinking that the bigger the dog the more credible the deterrent. However, intelligence is at least as important as size, which is why fox terriers are an excellent choice.

Step Three. Make sure there is a sofa, chair, or other platform in front of the window that gives a good vantage point from which to spot intruders. Since your dog will spend many hours at her post, I advise making the spot comfortable. It's the least that you can do.

Step Four. Get to know your dog's alert system. I have four levels. Some dogs may have only two or three. Regardless, you should know what your dog is alerting you to. What does a low growl mean? What does rapid barking mean? You should take the time to understand your dog.

Step Five. Pay attention to your dog! When she is on alert you should be too. Too many owners respond to a dog's alert by saying, "Fido, be quiet!" or "Quit barking! No!" And before you can say "No!" security is breached and trouble is imminent.

If you follow these five steps, you will be safe. Note that these steps apply to household security only. For advice on workplace security contact my brother, Freddy.

ACKNOWLEDGMENTS

Telling Rushie's story has been a profoundly enjoyable and liberating experience for me. As a lifelong academic, I've written my entire professional career. However, all my previous writing has been non-fiction, or as close to that as I could make it. Although I got satisfaction from my academic writing, *My Life* was a different and more enjoyable experience. I was able to focus on the writing itself–the structure and flow of the sentences and the coherence and entertainment value of the story. The emotional content of the writing was entirely novel. Academic writing strives to be emotionless. The opposite is true of fiction. Rushie was an emotional core of our lives for 14 years. I hope I have conveyed that adequately.

I relied on so many people for support and encouragement that it is impossible to name them all. Maury Baker, a fellow gym rat, provided valuable input and encouragement early in the process and the idea for the last chapter. I figured if a middle-aged fitness buff could find Rushie's story interesting, maybe there really was a market for the book.

Writing *My Life* took longer than I ever imagined. In that context, I'd like to thank my former boss JK: had she supported me as I supported her I'd never have had the time to finish the book.

Julia Potter, Diane Factor, Beverly Loyd, Joyce Feucht-Haviar, and Ken Dolan took the time to read an early draft and kept me motivated with encouraging comments and constructive criticism. My longtime friend, Jim Glass, a successful science fiction writer, read the manuscript and provided encouragement at a time when my enthusiasm was flagging. Michele Whitehead and Karalynn Ott provided detailed editorial and story suggestions, making the final version much better than it would have been otherwise. Linda Johnson read the revised manuscript and offered valuable comments. Linda Trevillion, the world's best proofreader, provided detailed editorial comments and I am sure her sharp eye saved me much personal embarrassment. My son's very talented friend, Suzanna Dikker, provided the wonderful illustrations.

I'd like to thank my long suffering relatives, particularly my mother, Laura Evans, and mother-in-law, Helen West, who cheerfully read several versions of the manuscript and nevertheless continued to offer support and encouragement. Most importantly I'd like to thank my wife, Natalie West, who provided constant encouragement, along with many insightful critiques. I would never have undertaken much less finished the book without her.

ABOUT THE AUTHOR

FRED EVANS is an educational consultant and writer. He spent much of his professional career as a professor and business school dean. During that time he contributed frequently to the academic press. *My Life* is his first biography. He is currently working on a book of short stories and a murder mystery where the protagonist's dog finds (and sometimes destroys) clues.

He divides his time between California, where he golfs and Utah where he skis. He is joined (on the ski slopes but not on the golf courses) by his wife, Natalie West. They share their homes with two dogs, a Welsh terrier, Prince Charles of Wales (Charlie) and a wire fox terrier, La Femme Nikita (Nikki).

www.ingramcontent.com/pod-product-compliance
Lightning Source LLC
Chambersburg PA
CBHW021241260626

47155CB00004BA/1256